"What do you know about love?"

Barrett raged on, "Or sex for that matter?"

"More than you think." Dani was uncomfortably conscious of the ruthless line of his mouth. "I know it takes two willing people."

"You believe that a man can't force himself on you," he jeered. "The first time I kissed you, I knew that if you had been kissed before, it wasn't by a man."

"I've been kissed before," Dani asserted.

She tried to push herself away from his chest, only to have him draw her more firmly against him. "Do you see how ?" Barre............................Now do you u...

"No,"...........................eyes briefly..............."No. Now I.................

JANET DAILEY AMERICANA

Every novel in this collection is your passport to a romantic tour of the United States through time-honored favorites by America's First Lady of romance fiction. Each of the fifty novels is set in a different state, researched by Janet and her husband, Bill. For the Daileys it was an odyssey of discovery. For you, it's the journey of a lifetime.

The state flower depicted on the cover of this book is goldenrod.

Janet Dailey Americana

Don't miss any of our special offers. Write to us at the following address for information on our newest releases.

Harlequin Reader Service
901 Fuhrmann Blvd., P.O. Box 1397, Buffalo, NY 14240
Canadian address: P.O. Box 603,
Fort Erie, Ont. L2A 5X3

Janet Dailey
Americana

BLUEGRASS KING

Harlequin Books

TORONTO • NEW YORK • LONDON
AMSTERDAM • PARIS • SYDNEY • HAMBURG
STOCKHOLM • ATHENS • TOKYO • MILAN

Janet Dailey Americana edition published February 1987
ISBN 373-89817-7

Harlequin Presents edition published September 1977
Second printing March 1980
Third printing April 1981

Original hardcover edition published in 1977
by Mills & Boon Limited

CHAPTER ONE

THE horses stomped restlessly in their stalls, straw rustling under their hooves. Sleek chestnut and bay heads were extended over their doors as they whickered softly at the rising crimson sun.

Dani Williams glanced over the back of the grulla, the mouse-grey stable pony she was saddling, her hazel eyes watching her father making his last-minute inspection of the tall, cedar-red Thoroughbred horse. Tension crackled in the air as the big horse bared his teeth and nipped at the stocky figure that was her father.

Muscles rippled in the powerful hindquarters as the horse edged away from the man, hooves moving lightly over the ground with the innate grace of a ballet dancer. A groom firmly held the halter of the bobbing equine head, occasionally being pulled nearly off the ground by the raising of the strong neck.

The Rogue—fierce and wild. Misbehaving for the sheer love of it. A fighter. But more important, The Rogue was a Thoroughbred racehorse. Dani's father had often said that if a man was lucky, he would see a horse like this once in his lifetime.

The marvel was that they owned him, this two-year-old stallion that stood nearly seventeen hands at the shoulder and still growing. Yet it wasn't The Rogue's bigness that promised greatness. There was the wide flare of the nostrils to drink in the wind, the broad chest to let the lungs fill to capacity and more precious than all, the nature-given desire to race.

The Rogue had raced three times as a two-year-old and three times he had won handily. The fourth time he went to the post, he never got out of the starting gate. Always fractious, always strong-willed, at race-time the big horse was an explosive keg of dynamite. His impatience had surfaced in his fourth race when he tried to open the starting gate himself and injured his right front leg in the process.

With a horse of The Rogue's calibre, no injury was slight. For two months they had babied, pampered, and nursed him along, taking no chances that would aggravate the bruise and muscle strain into something more serious. Today was the day The Rogue was to be tested.

A movement caught Dani's gaze, shifting it to the slender-built man walking towards her, a racing saddle over the arm that carried the riding crop. Her mouth moved in a tentative smile of greeting.

'I almost forget what it's like to get up at the crack of dawn,' he said, stopping beside her, his brown head failing by several inches to reach the top of her own.

'It's a nice quiet morning,' Dani murmured, smoothing her sweating palms over the sides of her faded jeans before preparing to tighten the saddle cinch. 'What do you think, Manny? Is he ready?'

Deep brown eyes were turned on Dani; like the dark complexion, they were a heritage of Manuel Herrera's Puerto Rican ancestry, but he gave her no answer. And Dani, who had spent nearly all of her nineteen years in the company of fragile racehorses, knew there was no certain answer to her question. At some point in a horse's full stride, all his thousand plus pounds was balanced on one leg whose ankle was no bigger around than that of a ballet dancer's.

A sigh shuddered from her lips in a vain attempt to relieve the tension that gripped her. With a fluid movement of long habit, Dani swung herself into the saddle of the stocky grey horse and walked him slowly to the larger, fidgeting Thoroughbred. The Rogue blew softly through his nose, nuzzling the neck of the more sedate horse, calming substantially while still moving nervously under the ministering hand of her father.

Her eyes searched the drawn lines of Lew Williams' face, missing none of the strain and tension that had him on edge, too. Lew Williams had once been a jockey like Manny, only he had lost the battle with his weight and height. But racing was in his blood. A few years after Dani was born, he had turned to training with mediocre success, then twelve years ago he had picked up his first horse in a claiming race.

But, as her father had often grumbled, it cost as much money to keep a loser as it did a winner, and most of the horses they had owned had been losers. Excluding The Rogue, they owned a string of six third-rate horses. The only money winner in the lot this year had been an ageing racing mare. But The Rogue—every dream her father had ever dreamed was wrapped up in this horse.

The bridle was on and the saddle was cinched. Her father boosted Manny into the saddle, then stared at the rider crouched like a monkey on the big horse's back.

'Once round the track at a canter to loosen him up,' Lew Williams instructed, his eyes running anxiously over the jockey's nodding head. 'Then a slow gallop, and dammit! I mean slow!' A swift glance encompassed Dani still mounted on the stocky mouse-grey. 'Take Nappy around with him. The Rogue will keep pace with him.'

The mouse-grey was his stablemate and the only horse The Rogue didn't attempt to outdistance. There was a brisk nod of understanding from Manny and a sharp glance directed at Dani, plainly saying she was to lead the way. Seconds later the pair were walking their horses on to the empty race track. For a furlong they trotted, paying no attention to the beautiful rose gardens in the infield. The famous twin spires of Churchill Downs clubhouse kept watch. Churchill Downs, home of the Kentucky Derby horse race, was more than a century old, patterned after the equally renowned Epsom Downs in England.

Neither rider said a word as Dani nudged the grey into a rocking canter and The Rogue followed suit. Around the oval track, the pair travelled clockwise once. Dani's stomach knotted as she urged the grey into a steady gallop, her gaze straining to pick up the slightest nuance that would indicate that the accompanying Rogue was favouring his right leg, but the big cedar-red stallion was effortlessly galloping beside her, pointed ears erect and swivelled forward as he tugged at the tightly wrapped reins without truly attempting to increase the pace.

As they drew level again with the stand where her father stood, Manny raised his whip to signal that all was well and Lew Williams motioned them to circle the track once more. At the end of the third route, he waved them to the gate.

Unconsciously Dani held her breath while she watched her father run his hand along the right front leg of the stallion. There was a watery brightness to his brown eyes as he looked up, a grin splitting the weathered lines around his mouth.

'He ain't even warm,' he said gruffly. And she knew the tightness in his voice was caused by the lump of relief in his throat. 'You might as well get down, Dani. The Rogue doesn't need a nursemaid any more.'

In compliance she slipped from the saddle, a hand reaching out to stroke the silken neck of The Rogue, then drawing quickly away when the finely boned head swung towards the hand, prepared to nip the unwary.

'You ill-tempered demon,' Dani crooned softly, smiling at the wide forehead with its darkly intelligent yet mischievous eyes. 'I'd almost let you bite me just to see you run again the way you were born to.'

But she stepped back, out of reach of his teeth, marvelling again at the magnificence of the animal before her. The perfectly carved head of The Rogue swung away from his admiring audience. Both Dani and her father turned to see what had captured his attention.

A golden chestnut was sidling towards them, a flaxen mane and tail, a white blaze down his forehead, and four flashing white stockings. Dani's smile hardened into grimness as she recognised the pride of Coronet Farm, Easy Doesit. Her hand moved in a masculine one-finger salute to the apprentice jockey astride the horse, Jimmy Graves, but her eyes dwelt coldly at the man striding effortlessly beside the trainer leading the horse, a man surrounded by an aura that suggested he had never been uncertain about anything in his life.

'Hello, Lew,' the man greeted her father. 'How's The Rogue today?'

'Barrett.' Her father's smile was broad and welcoming, a complete antithesis of his daughter's expression. 'He's every inch healthy.'

'He can take that movie horse of yours any day,' Dani declared, not attempting to hide the dry sarcasm in her voice.

'Hello, kid.' Cool green eyes flicked over her indifferently. 'Still as sassy as ever, I see.'

She half expected him to ruffle her hair, which was cropped in a short feminine version of a boy's cut that added little to the maturity of her face. As always her hair prickled along the back of her neck as she stared resentfully at Barrett King, but he was already ignoring her.

'Are you working this horse today, Lew, or are you only letting him get warm?' He was studying the restive movements of the horse, a glint of admiration in his gaze.

An exultant light glittered in Dani's eyes; she guessed how much Barrett King envied them the stallion he had tried to buy as a yearling from them. To this day her father declared that he had never considered selling The Rogue, but Dani knew how tempting the offer had been, especially in the face of steadily mounting feed bills, stable fees, and entry fees and four months without one of their horses finishing in the money. Twice he had picked up the telephone to accept Barrett King's offer, but she had managed to talk him out of it both times. Then the racing mare, Riding High, had providentially come in second. With the money in his pockets, the offer wasn't as tempting as the promise of the big stallion.

Yes, Dani was gloating now, knowing that they had a horse that all the King's money couldn't buy. And the King family, an old established family in the Bluegrass country of Kentucky, had a lot of money and only a pittance of it tied up in racehorses, but the ones they owned were the best. The fillies and colts that came from their stud farm in the heart of the Bluegrass were highly sought. There was immense satisfaction in watching Barrett King look at the stallion that any horseman would give his eye-teeth to own.

'I'm letting him go all out today, Barrett,' her father was saying. 'The Rogue works better with competition. What about it? Are you going to let Easy Doesit have his head?'

'Simms is the trainer,' the man shrugged, turning his easy smile to the man holding the golden chestnut. 'Do you want to run him alone or work him with The Rogue?'

'If you're afraid The Rogue is too much horse for yours,' Dani inserted with insidious softness, 'we'll understand.'

'Danielle.' The muttered reprimand from her father fortunately was meant only for her ears, but her taunt had brought Barrett King's gaze back to her. It angered her to notice that her words seemed to amuse him.

'We'll lead your horse once around the track,' the trainer Simms answered back, chuckling a bit as he spoke.

'We'll see who leads who!' Dani snapped, spinning abruptly on a booted heel and shoving her hands deep into the pockets of her faded jeans.

Anger gave impetus to her legs, carrying her quickly to the stand while her father and Barrett King followed at a more leisurely pace. Her smouldering gaze watched their progress, momentarily despising her father for showing such deference to the man at his side simply because he represented money.

From the first day she had seen Barrett King almost

five years ago, her hackles had raised. It had been the instant recognition of an enemy. Most people didn't see beyond the charming smile and the handsome façade, but Dani did. And she studied him again as he walked beside the short, paunchy figure that was her father.

He was tall, more than six feet, significantly dwarfing the men around the race-track, the breadth of his shoulders and depth of his chest slimmed down to a lean waist and hips, yet all were in keeping with his height.

Deep lines were etched in the sides of his mouth, amounting to masculine dimples. A grin quirked the corners and relieved the hint of fierceness from the powerful jaw and chin. His sternly handsome face was dominated by long, dark-lashed eyes of very vivid green. Yet these cool, reckless eyes always seemed to have little devils of laughter lurking in their clear depths. But Dani knew they were devils that could, if the occasion demanded it, leap to the front and become anything but laughter. Barrett King could be ruthless if he chose.

Thick masses of waving auburn hair crowned the top of his head, the fiery highlights accented by the morning sun. He was wearing a loden green sports suit, stitched in cream yellow like the pattern of his shirt opened at the throat. As always, he wore his clothes with careless grace. Her father classified him as a man's man, but Dani considered him a ladies' man, an opinion seemingly endorsed by the beautiful women who clustered around him.

At nineteen, Dani felt very worldly—not from experience but exposure. She had travelled the race-track circuit almost since she was born. For the first five years she had been accompanied by her mother, a woman who to this day she couldn't truly remember. Her mother had hated the unpredictable life of horse racing and had abandoned her husband and child. Dani was twelve when the word reached them that her mother had been killed in a car crash a few months before. Her father had grieved quietly, but she had felt nothing, a fact that had haunted her with overtones of guilt.

A frown dug deep furrows in her forehead. She loved racing. She loved horses. She didn't care two pins for the security her mother had craved. So they weren't wealthy like Barrett King, Dani thought angrily. So they lived out of the back end of a pick-up truck. This was her life and she loved it!

Up with the sun, the mornings were a joy. The scent of hay tickled her nose. The warm smell of horses. The combination of leather and saddle soap that always clung to her hands. The accelerated beat of her heart when the call to post was sounded. The mostly good-natured competition between horse owners. As for friends, she had hundreds scattered across the East Coast from Florida to New York.

So what if her clothes could all fit in one small suitcase and she didn't have a dress to her name? So what if the jeans and top that constantly adorned her slender figure made her look more like a young boy than a girl? So what if the only education she had known had come through the mail? So what if she dined mainly on hamburgers and Cokes? None of that made Barrett King any better than she was.

These last thoughts were the reason the glint in her eyes was so openly defiant when her father and Barrett King joined her. There was a puzzled question in the latter's eyes as he met her gaze, but as usual his glance never lingered very long on her. Barrett King saw her as a child, at most a teenager. That rankled with Dani, too. She wanted to declare that she was his equal, but the apprehensive light in her father's eye choked back the scathing comment that bubbled in her chest.

Clamping her lips shut, she turned her gaze track-ward to the two horses slowly circling the track counter-clockwise. Without the quieting influence of his stablemate, The Rogue was exhibiting the eager-ness to run, fighting the tight hold of the reins by the steel muscles of Manny's arms.

'He looks good, Lew,' Barrett commented.

'He looks more than good. He looks great!' Dani said firmly, the mediocre praise irritating her. 'When he's a three-year-old he's going to take the Triple Crown- -the Kentucky Derby, the Preakness, and then the Belmont.'

'It's not safe to count your chickens,' Barrett cautioned with a hint of mockery. 'The Rogue is only a horse.'

Her head spun around to glare at him angrily. 'You can say that because you haven't seen him run. You haven't seen The Rogue in full stride. Nothing can touch him. Nothing!' A brow was raised at her vehement declaration. 'You knew he was good, Mr King, that's why you tried to buy him, but he belongs to Lew and me!'

For once there were no devils in his cool, level gaze. 'It isn't good to become too attached to a horse, especially a working Thoroughbred. It can only lead to heartbreak—as it almost has already.'

'You'd like to see him crippled, wouldn't you?' she accused, her hazel eyes flashing cinnamon brown fires. 'If you can't have The Rogue, you don't want anyone else to have him either.'

'That will be enough.' Her father's voice was a low growl and just as menacing but the effect was dampened by the apologetic look he tossed to Barrett. 'You'll have to excuse my daughter. It's difficult to teach them the proper respect in this kind of environment.'

'I respect those who deserve it,' Dani retorted.

Her chin was tilted upward to indicate that the cool look she was receiving didn't intimidate her at all, but mentally she braced herself for the taller man's anger.

Instead Barrett said calmly, 'The horses are at the starting line.'

The decision had been made not to use the starting gate since The Rogue hadn't been worked out of it since his injury. At the signal from the trainer Simms, the two horses were off. The flashy chestnut immediately leaped to the front, a big agile horse except when compared with The Rogue. As they passed the trio in the stands, the cedar red Thoroughbred was at the chestnut's heels. Both horses were at a run, yet neither were at their top speed. The track was a mile round and races were won at the end, not the beginning.

'That's a tight wrap your jockey has on those reins.' The trainer Simms had joined them.

'The Rogue doesn't like other horses in front of him,' Lew explained, not taking his eyes off the racing horses now circling the track 'He tends to want to get in front too soon. We haven't been able to rate him.'

Around the first turn they ran, the pounding of their hooves overshadowing the pounding of Dani's heart. Along the backstretch The Rogue's nose had pulled even with the saddle of the golden chestnut. In a sense, it was a match race between the horse that the newspapers declared was the best three year-old and the horse that Dani knew was better than any three- or four-year-old. From under her thick brown lashes, she glanced surreptitiously at Barrett King.

'The Rogue is going to take your horse, you know,' she said softly and more than a little triumphantly.

His cool green gaze swept her face briefly but arrogantly, although he made no reply. As the horses came out of the final turn into the home stretch, Dani leaned forward her hands closing over the railing, their tight hold checking the cries that throbbed in her chest, screams of 'Go, Rogue, go!' All thought of the past injury to the big Thoroughbred were vanished from her mind. The chestnut's jockey was showing his horse the whip, flicking it near the side of the horse's head, but Manny had only relaxed his hold and was hand riding The Rogue, urging the horse to full stride.

Most horses quicken their stride to attain top speed as the chestnut was doing. Others, like The Rogue, lengthen their stride and are called striders. While Easy Doesit appeared to be giving it his all, The Rogue stretched out, magically flying above the ground, seeming to pass him with one bound and each effortlessly, gliding movement carried him farther ahead.

'I don't believe it,' Simms murmured in disbelief as The Rogue drew nearer the finish line- five, six lengths ahead of the flashy chestnut, still pulling away with his ears pricked forward under no strain at all.

'I told you!' Dani exclaimed, and turned away from the rail, exultant lights shining from her eyes. 'I told you nothing could touch him!'

Then came that sound, a short explosive pop that can be likened to no other sound, a small, insignificant sound that can turn the blood of any horseman to ice. Only one thing can make that sound—the snapping of a bone.

With a stifled cry, Dani spun back to the track, her wide, terrified eyes seeing the still galloping Rogue, his gait strange and uneven, the frantic efforts of Manny to pull the horse to a halt. Vaguely she was conscious of the three men vaulting over the railing and the movements of her own body to follow them as they raced down the dirt track to the gradually slowing horse and rider.

'He was sound. I swear to God he was sound. The leg was healed,' her father kept mumbling in what amounted to a desperate and disparaging prayer.

By the time they reached the horse, Manny had dismounted and was attempting to quiet the awkwardly prancing horse. The large intelligent eyes in the dished forehead of The Rogue were glazed as he struggled against the efforts of the four men to aid him. With nightmarish clarity, Dani watched the attempts of Barrett King to use his belt to cradle the leg of the dangling right ankle and prevent further damage being done.

Shock had rooted her to the ground until a piercing green gaze stabbed her. 'Get a vet, dammit!' Barrett commanded.

When she first turned to race towards the stables, her legs almost crumbled beneath her and for one horrified moment, Dani thought she was incapable of action. Then she was running, fighting back the sobs to gasp for breath.

There was no reality in the next thirty minutes. She couldn't consciously remember reaching Doc Langley's office on the race grounds, nor his clipped orders that sent his assistants scurrying to get the special horse van on the track. Vaguely Dani recalled the large hypodermic needle puncturing the cedar-red coat of The Rogue to sedate him, an indication that she must have accompanied the vet to the track. Snatches of conversation were jumbled in her mind, talk of X-rays and consulting Doctor Hamilton. Mostly there were grimly foreboding expressions.

When the daze lifted, Dani found her unseeing gaze was watching the slowly twirling racing goggles in the swarthy hand of Manny Herrera. A film of dust darkened his complexion except where the goggles had been. She was seated in a chair beside him, her fingers digging into the wooden arms. How she got there she had no idea. With an effort Dani raised her eyes from the hypnotic movement of the goggles, her nose registering the medicinal scent of the vet's office as her gaze spied the bowed head of her father.

'Lew?' Her voice was a plaintive whisper. She couldn't remember the last time she had called him Dad or Father.

When his greying head lifted, Dani saw the shattered, broken look in his eyes, the look of an old man who had suffered the final defeat, his spirit broken and his soul gone, leaving the hollow remnants of a man.

'His leg is broken,' his flat voice answered.

She had known that, but a violent shudder racked her slender body. With difficulty she swallowed the lump in her throat.

'That doesn't mean he has to be destroyed,' she asserted vigorously. Acid tears suddenly burned her eyes. 'Broken legs can be healed. It isn't hopeless!'

But her father only looked on her blankly and lowered his head in his hands.

'Remember when Swaps broke his leg.' The words were a plea not to give up. 'The doctors can fix The Rogue, too. You'll see. He'll race again, I know it. I know it!'

The door opened and Doctor Langley walked in. 'Lew.' The vet's gaze met none of the others in the room, settling immediately on the man hunched forward in his chair.

'Yes.' Her father's voice seemed to come from some deep, empty cavern as he acknowledged the man without raising his head.

'Hamilton and I have studied the X-rays thoroughly. There isn't any hope.' The blunt sentence was deliberately clipped as the raw edges of his tone sawed through the air.

Dani stared at the elderly doctor in disbelief. Her head moved in a sharp negative movement to the side as if to shake off his verdict. Then her father's tight voice sliced the room.

'Do what you have to do.'

Dr Langley started to turn back to the door. Dani bounded to her feet.

'No!' she shrieked. 'There must be something you can do. You aren't going to destroy The Rogue!'

'I'm sorry.' The vet's expression was sadly firm as he reluctantly brought his gaze to bear on Dani. 'There's nothing left of his ankle bones but a thousand tiny fragments.'

A trembling rage took possession of her. She refused to accept his statement. Her breath was coming in quick, painful spasms as her head kept moving from side to side.

'I don't believe you,' she said hoarsely.

Her mind vaguely registered the pitying glances of other commiserating horsemen in the room. There was a movement in the doorway and Barrett King entered the room, tall and compelling. Resentment boiled as she saw the rueful nod of the vet in Barrett's direction, answering the unasked question that was evidently in the green eyes.

'You're to blame for this.' Dani turned her trembling temper on the auburn-haired man. 'How much did you pay him to have The Rogue destroyed? You tried to buy him and we wouldn't sell.' Her shaking legs traversed the short distance to stand in front of him, her head thrown back, tears glimmering in the corners of his eyes. 'You got your revenge, didn't you? They're going to kill him! They're going to kill him!'

Her tight fists began pummelling his chest, beating against the solid wall with all her strength. Lights exploded around her, then hands were closing over her arms trying to draw her away from him, but distantly, she heard Barrett King's voice saying, 'Let her be.' And the hands let her go.

Slowly her cries of anger and hatred gave way to sobs of pain and anguish. Beneath her, Dani felt her knees begin to buckle before a pair of strong arms slipped around in support and she was drawn against that hard wall she had tried to knock down.

'Go ahead, kid,' a comforting voice said near her ear. 'Cry it all out.'

Behind her eyes, there were more explosions of light and she sobbed wildly, hearing nothing but the steady beat behind the wall and the racking sounds in her throat. As the force of her grief began to subside, she heard a door close. Opening her tear-drenched eyes, she focused her gaze beyond the loden green material around her and on her father. A man was standing beside him. She couldn't say how she knew, but some inner voice told her he was the consultant vet, Dr Hamilton.

Dani didn't need to see the sudden crumpling of her father to know that the man had come to tell him it was over. The Rogue was dead. Her hands crept to her ears, as if covering them would prevent the news reaching her. She heard someone scream 'No!' then realised it came from herself. Then there was a strange buzzing in her ears and waves of blackness washed over her while strong arms tightened their hold.

CHAPTER TWO

THE bed was strange and totally unfamiliar. Dani blinked and glanced around the room, trying to remember which hotel they were staying in this time. One glance at the sterile walls and the crisp sheets covering her told her she was in a hospital. Mentally she checked out her body to discover where she was hurt, only to decide that the only thing troubling her was the throbbing in her head.

Had The Rogue kicked her? she wondered. A nauseous wave consumed her as she remembered The Rogue was dead, mercifully destroyed because he had shattered the bones in his ankle. With a painful moan, she turned her head into the starched pillows and let the tears slip from her hazel eyes. But she didn't cry nor sob, despite the dull, disbelieving ache in her heart.

Twisting her head back, she stared unblinkingly at the snow-white ceiling, not bothering to wipe the fresh tears from her cheeks and not caring how tousled her short brown hair was because of the way she had pushed her head back against the pillow. Footsteps sounded near her door, slow defeated footsteps. Before they entered her room, she knew they belonged to her father.

'Hello, Danielle,' her father greeted quietly. No smile turned up the corners of his mouth and there was no light in his eyes.

'Hello, Lew,' she answered.

An uneasy silence came between them. A week ago she wouldn't have given a thought to how old her father was. Now, looking at the small, broken man, she tried to remember if he was fifty-six or fifty-seven. He looked much older than that.

'Why am I here?' she asked finally.

'You collapsed. The shock of ... of ...'

His voice broke again and Dani didn't force him to say the words. 'I see,' she murmured. 'When can I leave?'

'They want you to stay overnight. It's the best thing —considering,' he sighed.

'Considering what? I'm all right now.'

'You might as well take advantage of the peace and quiet while you can,' her father said cryptically, his unnaturally pale face caught her questioning look. 'There were a bunch of newspaper reporters at the vet's. Your picture and Barrett King's are plastered all over the paper.'

Then Dani remembered those strange explosions of light that had seemed so much a part of the nightmare of her memory. Obviously they had been flashbulbs. She shrunk inwardly at the recollection of her attack on Barrett King and the vile accusations she had made.

Logically she could reason that her attack had been caused by the need to strike back—at anyone. Her total dislike of Barrett King had made him the likely choice. She felt no regret for what she had done, only that it had been witnessed by outsiders. She tried to catch her father's gaze, but he refused to meet hers.

'Why do you hate him so much?' he sighed.

Her quick retort was instinctive. 'Because he breathes.' Normally her sharp wit would have brought a reluctant smile to her father's face, but this time his head moved wearily in despair. 'I'm sorry, Lew,' Dani spoke hesitantly, her chin lowering itself to rest on her chest. 'That man simply rubs me the wrong way.'

'I wish we would have sold The Rogue to him.'

'What are you saying?' She gasped in sharply at her father's traitorous statement. Her head jerked upward as she tried to fathom the blank expression of the man gazing sightlessly at the drawn curtains of the hospital window.

'Your mother was right about me.' He ignored her question and continued speaking in that same emotionless tone. 'If I entered a one-man race, I'd lose. I'm a loser. I wasn't any good as a jockey. Only fools hired me to train their horses. Those hayburners we own aren't fit to be called Thoroughbreds. A man like me had no right to own The Rogue.'

'No!' But her whispering protest was for his self-flagellation.

'It's the truth.' Brown eyes were turned on Dani. Mirrors of the soul, they had been called. There was no reflection, just deep, bottomless pools of brown intensified by the sunken hollows surrounding them. 'I was given a spirited young filly to raise—you, Dani. And what did I do? I gave you free rein. I never tried to curb you or control your fiery temper. I even ignored the rudiments of grooming. You aren't to blame for the way you acted today. I am.'

Tears began to scald her eyes again. 'Don't say things like that!'

'What do you know, girl? Horses, that's all you know,' he answered for her. 'You eat, sleep, and smell like horses. You don't know what it is to be a woman or a lady. How could you? You've never known any.'

Dani watched in horrified silence as a shaking hand reached inside the jacket of his worn suit. Wide, frightened eyes saw the crumpled wad of bills being pushed towards her, shoved by cold fingers into her resisting palm.

'When you leave the hospital tomorrow morning, I don't want you to come to the track. I don't want you to go near one ever again.' His voice was trembling as badly as his hands, but the fervour in it was undeniable. 'I want you to take this money and make a new life for yourself. Get an apartment, a job, or go to school. Live like a normal person, not a gypsy.'

'Where did you get this?' she demanded hoarsely as the folded bills flipped open and she realised there was at least two or three thousand dollars in her hand.

'I sold the horses . . . all except the mare. All I know is racing. I don't know anything else,' he mumbled brokenly. 'But you're young. You can make a new start, a new life.' A tear trickled out of the corner of his eye, unnoticed. 'You're a fighter—like The Rogue. You can be something. But not if you stick with me. I'll drag you down and you'll be a nothing, a loser just like me.'

'No, Daddy, no!' She scurried forward, her hands reaching out for him, unconscious that she had not called him Lew, but he drew back from the bed.

'Promise me you'll have nothing to do with horses. They'll break your heart and your spirit. Promise me.'

27

'I promise.' She shook her head firmly, almost blinded by tears.

'I'm leaving tonight. I don't know where I'm going or when I'll see you again,' he continued absently. 'The track is crawling with reporters. I can't stand to talk about ...' For a long minute, his eyes rested on her bewildered face. 'Goodbye, Dani.'

Before she realised it, he had left the room. She tried to call him back, but she couldn't get anything to come out of her knotted muscles in her throat. Clutching the money in her hand, she pushed back the sheet and scrambled to her feet, the bottom of the hospital gown flapping strangely around her bare knees. No longer stunned by his announcement, she felt the need to go after her father and convince him that nothing he said was true.

Racing towards the small closet in the room, Dani was halted by the sight of a slender girl in a white gown hurrying towards her. It took a full second before she realised it was a mirror reflecting her own image.

Short, short hair was a richly glowing brown in the overhead light. The cinnamon shade of her hazel eyes was enhanced by her thick but not long lashes. Ignoring the boyish style of her hair, Dani noticed for the first time the clean lines of her face, oval with nicely prominent cheekbones, a small and straight nose above a well-shaped mouth and naturally arched eyebrows. Her neck was long and graceful, like a race-horse's. The skin of her arms and face was a light golden colour, showing no inclination to freckle.

But her legs were pale white beneath the gown, never having been exposed to the sun the way her face and arms were. They were slender, yet well muscled. In fact, she thought, as she hitched the hospital gown up near her thighs, her legs looked quite similar to those of the scantily clad girls on the calendars at the stables. This was the first time she had attempted to assess her figure in comparison to other feminine forms, and she realised she was quite shapely with her gently rounded hips and nipped-in waist.

'You have very beautiful legs. How old are you?'

At the sound of the curious masculine voice, Dani let go of the gown, letting the hem fall down around her knees as she spun to face the man leaning against the door jamb.

'Who are you? What do you want?' Her cheeks flamed as she encountered the unabashed look of dark, dark brown eyes.

'Marshall Thompsen,' the stranger replied smoothly. A brow as thick and as black as his hair arched above one eye as his gaze travelled lazily over her. 'Barrett said you were a child.'

Dani had concealed her hands behind her back to hide the money she still clutched, unaware that the action tightened the thin cotton gown across her front, outlining the upward thrust of her breasts.

'I am not a child!' she retorted firmly.

'I can see that,' he murmured with a smile that was obviously meant to charm.

'What are you doing here?' She began to edge warily towards the bed. 'If Barrett King sent you, then you can just turn around and leave.'

'Hardly, my love. The redoubtable Mr King and I cannot be referred to as friends by any stretch of the imagination. Acquaintances, enemies even, but never friends.' The man straightened and stepped further into the room. 'I was curious to see the little female David who was able to subject Barrett to such vitriolic abuse without suffering his retribution.'

'Are you one of those reporters?' Dani accused, her fingers reaching for the telephone at her bedside.

Her continued resistance to his practised charm didn't seem to disconcert him a bit. 'You do crush a man's ego! I'm not a reporter, although I do possess a slim claim to fame as a syndicated columnist, a running chronicle of the lives—and loves—of the socially elite.'

'That still isn't an answer as to what you're doing here,' Dani persisted.

'I thought I'd already explained.' A gold cigarette case materialised in the hand that had been in the pocket of his impeccably tailored blazer. 'Barrett King is always good material, and that was quite a scene the two of you must have had this morning.'

'Were you there?' she demanded.

'I only know what I read in the newspapers.' A cigarette was now lit and the smoke curling near his black hair. From under his arm, he withdrew a copy of a newspaper and handed it to her. 'Have you seen it?'

'No.' Her head moved briefly in a negative gesture as she accepted the paper, sliding on to the bed and discreetly slipping the money beneath her pillow.

Her father had told her about the article, but Dani had imagined some small write-up, possibly with a picture tucked in some hidden corner of the paper. She hadn't expected the story would monopolise nearly one entire page. There were three photographs. The largest was of her impotent attempt to beat him with her fists. The second picture must have been taken after she collapsed because it showed her being carried in Barrett King's arms. But the last brought a tight knot of pain in her chest. There was The Rogue, a magnificent photo taken of him rearing and fighting off a groom who was trying to hold him. Dani remembered it had been taken some months before, during the saddling of his third race. He looked so invincible. It hurt unbearably to remind herself that The Rogue was dead.

A frown covered her face to fight back the scalding tears as she glanced at the handsome man identified as Marshall Thompsen. 'Why?' she asked huskily. 'Why all this? Nobody's even heard of The Rogue before.'

'It was a combination of things, I imagine,' he shrugged, the darkness of his eyes not hiding the sharpness of his gaze nor concealing the shrewdness behind his suave exterior. 'A lack of any other noteworthy news, the human interest angle of a possibly great horse being destroyed, and the name of Barrett King. I don't suppose there was any truth in your accusations?'

Dani's chin lifted defiantly, her eyes sparkling with anger and unshed tears. 'He wanted The Rogue. He tried to buy him, but we wouldn't sell. My father——' Her voice trailed off, unwilling to relate her father's assertion that they should have sold the Thoroughbred to Barrett King, that they had no right to own a horse like The Rogue.

'Yes, I saw your father slipping out of your room and down the back stairs. That was how I was able to guess which room was yours.' The man smoothly filled in the gap left by her uncompleted sentence, allowing her time to regain her control. 'No doubt he was trying to avoid the queue of reporters hovering about the entrance. He isn't taking The Rogue's death very well, is he?'

The quiet probing question struck a responsive chord in Dani and she was suddenly overcome with a need to confide the confusing turn of events that had taken place. Her words tumbled over each other as she quickly explained how severely depressed her father was, of his insistence that he was a failure, a loser, even his assertion that they should have sold The Rogue to Barrett King and why She glossed over the part about his lack of paternal guidance with her and omitted any mention of the money tucked under her pillow after all, she wasn't totally ignorant of the lengths some men would go to separate herself from that sum of money—and she ended her tale with the fact that Lew had pushed her out on her own while he left town that very night. Her only reaction from Marshall Thompsen was the brilliant gleam that glittered in his dark eyes.

'You never did say how old you were?' he commented, unnaturally interested in the burning tip of his cigarette.

'Nineteen. I'll be twenty in November.'

'That's certainly old enough to leave the nest. What do you plan to do?'

'I thought,' Dani inhaled deeply, 'I thought I would go after my father. He shouldn't be alone at a time like this.'

'From a man's point of view, I think you're wrong. He's evidently convinced himself that he's a failure as a father as well as a man. For you to go chasing after him with your well-meaning pity would only enforce his opinion. There are times when a person, male or female, needs to be by themselves to work things out and not use anyone else as a crutch. This could be one of those times for your father.'

'So you think I should do as he asked?' she said thoughtfully, appreciating the logic of his reasoning. 'The only problem is,' she sighed, 'what am I going to do? Lew made me promise I wouldn't have anything to do with horses, and that's all I know.'

'Has anyone ever told you— Dani, isn't it?'

'Yes, short for Danielle,' she supplied.

'I like that name,' Marshall Thompsen murmured.

'It has class. Has anyone told you that you're photogenic?'

'What does that mean?' Again the wariness crept back in her voice.

'It means that you look attractive in photographs.' His long fingers made a deprecating gesture towards her bluntly short hair. 'Excluding that butchered hairstyle and those boys' clothes you wear, your face is very expressive in pictures. You could become a model, although there's an over-abundance of young women aspiring to such a position.'

'Are you offering to make me one?' Dani asked, looking sceptically at the handsome man now.

'Oh, I could under the right circumstances,' he answered without the slightest hesitation.

'And what kind of circumstances would that be? Stopping at your apartment around midnight to view some of your sketches?' she demanded sarcastically.

'Your mind is as swift and as sharp as your tongue,' he chuckled softly.

'I may not be sophisticated, but neither am I naïve, Mr Thompsen.'

'Marshall,' he corrected. 'And I'll call you Danielle. An evening at my apartment was not the circumstances I had in mind, although I'm sure it would be enjoyable. No, I have an even better plan, one that Barrett King may not like, but I think you and I will.'

'What is it?'

He glanced at his watch, large, gold and expensive like everything else he wore. 'The nurse will be coming any moment and your room is strictly off limits. I won't have time to explain it now. You're to be released in the morning, aren't you?'

'Yes,' Dani nodded, puzzled by his conspiratorial air and more than a little curious about what he had in mind.

Again his hand reached into the pocket that contained the gold cigarette case, only this time it drew out a business card which he handed to her.

'Call me tomorrow after you've left the hospital and we'll get together to discuss it.' White teeth flashed when he smiled. 'At a public restaurant of your choosing,' he added with a wink as he started towards the door. 'It would be better if you didn't mention my visit to Barrett when you see him.'

'I won't be seeing him, so there's little likelihood that he'll find out,' Dani replied waspishly.

'Don't you know?' The dark brow arched again in a mocking movement. 'This is an exclusively private hospital and Mr King is picking up the tab for your stay. You can be sure he'll be in to see you some time before you're released.'

With that bombshell of information Marshall Thompsen left the room. Dani spluttered silently, having no one to vent her rage on, then settled back against the bed as she planned what she would say to Barrett King when she saw him. The lump of money beneath her pillow reassured her that she wasn't a charity case and there would be considerable pleasure in informing Mr King.

'Well, I see you've finally woken. How are you feeling?' A white-uniformed nurse walked briskly into the room, a smile fixed on her round face.

After her initial start of surprise, Dani recovered and answered calmly, 'I'm fine, thank you.'

Silently she endured the taking of her temperature, pulse and blood pressure which the nurse performed with businesslike efficiency, half listening to the remarks made about the stir Dani had caused with the press.

'You slept through lunch and dinner,' the nurse stated after she had entered the results on Dani's chart. 'Would you like some sandwiches and milk?'

Sandwiches and milk. Dani hid the wry smile that tugged at the corners of her mouth. If the nurse had offered milk and cookies, she couldn't have indicated more clearly that she believed herself to be speaking to a child. But the suggestion made her realise there was an empty gnawing in her stomach.

'Yes, I am hungry,' she admitted.

'I'll be right back with a tray,' the nurse smiled, and returned a few minutes later. But before the nurse left again, she showed Dani how to operate the buzzer at her bedside and added, 'If you have trouble getting to sleep, the doctor authorised us to administer a sleeping pill. I'll come back later to pick up your tray.'

With the nurse's departure, Dani unwrapped the first sandwich and began eating hungrily, spreading out the newspaper to read the article beneath her pictures. The first few paragraphs she skimmed over since they dealt with the factual happenings of the morning with a brief reference to The Rogue's previous winning record and the muscle injury he had sustained that had kept him out of the bigger races.

The sandwich became tasteless as she read Manny's account of this morning's workout and his statement that the track had been in excellent condition and The Rogue had shown no favouritism at all to his previous injury. His conclusion was a freak misstep on the Thoroughbred's part. Her throat tightened at the glowing words of praise from the jockey when he told of the supreme effort The Rogue had made to keep from falling and perhaps causing more injury to himself as well as Manny. Yet Dani knew that the very fact that The Rogue hadn't gone down had also contributed to the irreparable damage done to his ankle.

There was a synopsis of her father's career in racing, even his stint as a jockey before his weight had forced his retirement. Comments from the track people Dani knew referred to her as an emotional and sensitive young girl and blamed her highly spirited nature as the cause for her blow-up at Barrett King when she had learned of the eminent destruction of The Rogue.

Lew Williams had refused to make any comment on the reporter's questions, a fact duly noted in the article. But there were quotes from Barrett King, and Dani read them with a grim sort of eagerness.

In reply to the question what was the truth behind her accusations, Barrett had admitted, 'I attempted to buy the colt from Williams as a yearling because I

37

thought it had potential. Lew said he would consider the offer although his daughter told me outright that The Rogue wasn't for sale. A few days later, her father told me the same thing. I held no ill-feelings because of his decision. In his place, I would have done the same thing. The girl was obviously very attached to the horse, as young people tend to be. I suppose I represented some kind of threat, which was why she lashed out at me today. She was overwrought—certainly in no condition to be held responsible for her actions.'

Barrett's comment as to his assessment of The Rogue's ability was: 'My horse, Easy Doesit, has faced some pretty stiff competition this year and come out on top most of the time. Today The Rogue crossed the finishing line six lengths ahead and still pulling away easily. He might have been the horse of the decade, as you newspapermen like to call them, but that's something we shall never know for certain.'

The article concluded with the bitter sentence that The Rogue had broken down during a workout and was destroyed without ever reaching his prime.

Dani gulped down her milk, trying to swallow the lump in her throat at the same time. She shifted her gaze to the photographs again, studying them with more than passing interest this time as she tried to gauge Barrett King's reaction by his expression.

In the first picture, the strong line of his jaw was emphasised as if clenched. There was an arrogant tilt of his head and the look in his eyes was indecipherable, but his arms were at his side as he allowed himself to be subjected to the pathetic punishment of her fists.

In the second, he was carrying her in his arms, effortlessly striding towards the camera. This time there was no mistaking the grim expression on his face—whether from concern or anger, Dani had no way of telling. In that picture she did look young and immature, unconscious in his arms, her head resting against his chest.

The memory of the warmth and the strength she had felt in those arms only moments before she had lost consciousness came rushing back, an embrace that had seemed to absorb some of her anguish. There had been so much security and comfort in that low voice that had urged her to cry.

Comfort? She nearly snorted the word aloud. What a strange word to associate with an overbearing person like Barrett King. Never would she be able to conceive a time when she could be comfortable in his arms.

Angrily she thrust the newspaper away from her. She refused to think about him any more.

CHAPTER THREE

AFTER breakfast the next morning, Dani scrambled into her boots, faded jeans, and the shapeless blouse that transformed her slender, feminine figure into one of boyish slimness. At the sound of firm footsteps in

39

the hallway outside her door, a sixth sense warned her that Marshall Thompsen's prophecy that she would see Barrett King before she left the hospital was about to come true. When his voice greeted her from the doorway, her face didn't register any surprise.

'Good morning,' she replied crisply, casting a defiant glance at him before reaching in her back pocket for the comb she always kept there. The hairs along the back of her neck were tingling, sending a thousand tiny vibrations through her body.

'How are you feeling this morning?'

Dani refused to let the warmth in his voice charm her as it did so many others. She saw through him.

'I'm quite recovered,' she answered.

To her relief, a nurse walked into the room. Young and attractive, she made a quick and effusive apology to Barrett for interrupting them. When she glanced at Dani, it was almost an afterthought.

'There were a few details about you, Miss Williams, that we weren't able to obtain when you were admitted yesterday,' the nurse explained. 'We do need them for our records in the event you have the misfortune to come here again.'

The last was obviously meant as a small joke since the nurse laughed after she said it. But Dani didn't smile as she glanced at Barrett, wishing he would leave and knowing he wouldn't.

'What is it you need to know?' she asked instead, her mouth tightening as she watched Barrett walk to the window of her room.

The data the nurse required consisted of details of her childhood diseases, permanent residence, and her date of birth. As the information was all noted on the nurse's pad, Dani noticed the way the young woman's gaze continued to stray to Barrett. Only once did she herself look to see if he was watching them, but he was still staring out of the window, the sunlight streaming in to accent the coppery shade of his thick hair. It irritated her the way his presence could dominate a room.

The nurse smiled. 'That's everything. The doctor will be here within the hour to release you formally.'

Dani wasn't deceived. She knew the smile was really meant for Barrett, and she pitied the nurse for being taken in by the striking looks and not seeing the ruthlessness that lay behind those catlike green eyes.

'Why did you lie, Dani?' Barrett demanded as he turned a censorious gaze on her.

There was a sparkle of anger in her eyes. 'I didn't lie! You wanted The Rogue for yourself!'

'I'm not talking about that.' The sharpness was out of his tone, but the underlying hardness was still there. 'I'm referring to just now. I know it must seem an incredibly long time before you're an adult, but lying about your age won't help you reach it any faster.'

'I wasn't lying. I'm nineteen and I shall be twenty in November! I'm sorry I can't produce a birth certificate on the spur of the moment to prove it,' she retorted sarcastically.

There was something very insolent about the way

his level gaze swept her from head to toe. It was all she could do not to reach out for the pitcher of water and throw it at him.

'You don't look a day over fifteen,' he murmured.

'Spare me the "sweet sixteen and never been kissed" remarks,' she snapped. 'I am not sixteen and I assure you I have been kissed.'

'Not very thoroughly.' There were wicked devils of laughter dancing in his eyes.

Her hands moved to a defiant stance on her hips, reminding her at the same moment that the bulge in her pocket was made by the money her father had given her and Marshall Thompsen's statement that Barrett intended to pay for her hospital stay. Before she could mention it, and her intention to take care of her own expenses, he spoke again.

'Have you seen your father?'

'Why?' deliberately and guardedly answering his question with one of her own.

'I stopped at the track to talk to him this morning and discovered he was gone. It seems he left last night. Do you know anything about it?' His head was tilted inquiringly to one side.

'Yes,' Dani answered simply.

A muscle jumped along his jawline and Dani knew her lack of further explanation angered him. With reluctant admiration, she noticed the control that kept his temper in check.

'Will he be here this morning when you're released?' he asked with marked patience.

'No.'

'Instead of playing twenty questions, why don't you explain to me what the situation is?' His penetrating gaze was formidable with its demand and Dani had difficulty meeting it.

'Is that what we were playing?' she asked with mock innocence. 'I'm never quite sure what your game is.' She knew the snide comment hadn't gone unnoticed as she hurried on. 'The situation is simply: my father left town last night. He left some money with me to take care of the hospital bill.' She extracted two large bills from the roll in her pocket and waved them in the air for his confirmation.

'That's been taken care of already.' Barrett spoke with ominous quietness.

'We Williams' don't need your charity—or is it really a twinge of guilty conscience?' she chided, letting the sarcasm flow freely.

He took two quick strides forward, his tallness suddenly looming over her. 'It was a gesture of sympathy on my part. I feel no guilt over the loss of your horse. As you very well know, I had no part in it.'

Dani had the honesty to redden at his subtle reference to her accusation the day before. 'No, I know you didn't,' she admitted, although through gritted teeth, hating to have him right about anything. 'I suppose I should apologise for the things I said.'

As swiftly as it had come, his anger vanished. 'Don't apologise if you don't mean it.' Laughter rang in his voice, mocking her reluctant admission.

'Well, I will,' Dani asserted, her chin lifting rebelliously. 'I'm sure there are enough things that can be said about you that are true without resorting to lying.'

'I accept your backhanded apology,' Barrett smiled.

His head moved in a mocking nod and she was forcibly reminded of his magnetism. There was no mistaking the virility behind the teak-carved exterior. Barrett King was a potent combination of looks, wealth, and charm. Dani turned away, silently grateful that she was immune to such things. She swallowed back the slight attack of breathlessness that had caught hold of her throat at his sweeping glance.

'Are you planning to rejoin your father immediately?' he asked quietly.

'Why?' Her question was wary, as were all her reactions to him.

'I think it would be best if you waited a couple of days before attempting to travel.' Indifference lined his voice.

'There's nothing wrong with me. I only fainted,' she reminded him.

She had no intention of telling Barrett that she would not be joining her father, nor was she going to mention Marshall Thompsen, not because of his suggestion, but because it was none of Barrett's business. However, she was wise enough to realise that as long as Barrett remained the inquisitor the chance that she might let her plans slip was increased.

'Why are you here?' she demanded with a suddenness that was supposed to catch him off guard.

'To offer my help,' he answered without any hesition. The cool, level gaze was difficult to meet.

'What would I need your help for?' Her tone was deliberately derisive, trying to counteract the sensation that he was winning their imaginary battle.

'For starters, there are a couple of reporters waiting downstairs——'

'And you're afraid I'll make more inflammatory remarks about you, I suppose,' Dani jeered.

'You can say anything you like to them,' Barrett said quietly but with a grimness that suggested underlying temper. 'I thought since your father had seen fit to run away from them that perhaps you weren't very anxious to see them yourself.'

'My father ran away from himself, not the reporters,' she corrected, and immediately wished she could bite off her tongue at the sharply questioning look he gave her. 'And I'm very capable of dealing with a few nosey men without any assistance from you, so you can leave any time you want. The sooner the better as far as I'm concerned,' arrogantly arching a brow in his direction.

'Very well,' was his clipped reply as the broad back was turned towards her and he started for the open door.

'And, Mr King——' Her eyes glittered with defiant triumph as the auburn head turned in answer to his name, 'I shall be paying for my stay here. Whatever arrangements you've made to the contrary can be cancelled.'

There was a grim line to his mouth and jaw as he surveyed her with unnerving thoroughness. Her heartbeat quickened.

'Have you ever seen an unruly horse saddled and bridled, Miss Williams?' Barrett continued, with the certainty that Dani had seen it many times. 'His tongue is held to keep him in line. I wonder how it would work with a headstrong brat like you?'

While she gasped in outraged anger, Barrett King walked calmly from the room. Seething with impotent fury, she stalked about the room, muttering savage imprecations and kicking out at the chair and bed, suffering the consequences of a stubbed toe. When the doctor arrived to release her formally, it was he who suffered the rough edge of her tongue.

At the cashier's counter on the first floor, Dani drew herself up to her full height of five foot four inches and demanded her bill, fully prepared to argue her right to pay it. Surprisingly, the elderly woman produced it without comment, taking most of the wind from Dani's stormy sails. With the receipt tucked in her pocket with the rest of the money her father had given her, Dani entered the lobby of the hospital.

All hope that she could slip past the reporters unnoticed fled when she saw the emptiness of the room. That, combined with her apparel of faded blue jeans, boots, and the disreputable blouse, brought everyone's attention to her immediately. Squaring her shoulders,

Dani attempted to brazen her way across the tiled floor, but three men and a photographer surrounded her, bombarding her with questions and denying her a clear path to the door.

'Could you tell us where your father is, Miss Williams?'

'What is your reaction to Mr King's comment that the true worth of The Rogue will never be known? Do you agree with him?'

'What are your plans now, Miss Williams?'

'Would you look this way, miss?'

Her hand shielded her face from the flashing of another bulb. 'Please let me through.' She was forced to raise her voice to make herself heard over their barrage of questions. 'Let me by!'

But her requests were ignored and her hazel gaze searched wildly for some other means of escape, but the men had her blocked at every turn. Beyond the shoulder of one man Dani saw the mocking smile of Barrett King as he leaned against a far wall. The deeply grooved corners of his mouth showed his obvious amusement at her predicament. For a split second, her eyes begged for his help before she turned determinedly away.

'Let me through,' she repeated in a desperate tone as she tried to push her way around one of the men, who merely took a step backward without providing any opening at all.

In the next second, Dani felt a firm hand grip her elbow and she turned towards it almost in relief.

'Come on, fellers, give the girl a break,' Barrett's amused yet authoritative voice was saying. 'She may have been released from the hospital, but no girl can fend off a pack of wolves, especially when they attack en masse!'

'We only want to ask her a few questions, Barrett,' one of the reporters said in a wheedling tone.

'Do you want to answer them?'

From the direction of his voice, Dani knew Barrett had bent his head towards her. 'I just want to get out of here,' she muttered into his shirt front.

'You heard the lady, Fred,' Barrett said lightly, his arm moving around her shoulders as the reporters, surprisingly, stepped aside, grumbling goodnaturedly but acquiescing to the steel softness in his voice.

Dani wanted to run out of the front door, but the arm around her shoulders kept her firmly at Barrett's side as they walked unhurriedly across the lobby and through the doors. On the hospital steps, she turned to thank him for his help even as she resented the necessity for doing so. But he propelled her down the steps, turning her towards the parking lot.

'I can make it on my own now, thank you,' she stated, shrugging herself free of his arm. 'I don't need your help any more.'

His fingers slipped to her wrist, holding her when she would have walked away. His superior strength forced her to stay.

'In two minutes those reporters would find you and you would be in the same predicament as before.' His mouth curved in a complacent and humourless smile as he studied the mutinous expression on her face. 'I know it goes against the grain, but if you want to avoid them, you'll have to accept a ride from me.'

With her lips pursed in an angry line, she glared at him, angry that she hadn't been able to extract herself from the reporters without his help. And worse, he was taking delight in rubbing her nose with that fact. He was entirely too sure of himself.

'Where's your car?' Dani snapped churlishly, turning away from the green eyes that made her feel small and silly.

He gestured towards a racy, cream-yellow sports car parked next to the kerb, sleek and low to the ground, and Dani knew she would be forced to sit disgustingly close to this arrogant man. His attitude, as he ceremoniously opened the car door for her, was deliberately cavalier, a jibe at her own lack of manners. She hugged the door as tightly as possible while he walked around to the other side.

'Where do you want to go?' he asked, darting an amused glance while he started the motor and put the car in gear.

The muscles in her body tensed as she tried to think of a destination. To request that he leave her at a bus stop would only arouse his curiosity at her reluctance to tell him where she wanted to go. And hesitating too long before answering him would achieve the same thing. Quickly she told him the name of a small café near the race-track.

'Don't you want to go to your hotel?' he asked curiously.

'Not right away.' Dani kept her gaze firmly fixed on the road ahead. 'I . . . I made arrangements to meet a friend at the café.'

Under the cover of one hand, she crossed her fingers. It was a half-truth since she intended to telephone Marshall Thompsen to arrange a meeting with him. She sensed that Barrett didn't altogether believe her and expected him to probe further into her statement. Bracing herself to put him firmly in his place if he did, Dani was surprised when he fell into a thoughtful silence that lasted the short distance from the hospital to the café.

When he pulled up to the kerb, her hand automatically reached for the handle of the door, anxious to be away. But his quietly spoken voice halted her.

'I'm sorry about The Rogue. I hope you believe me,' Barrett said quietly.

She glanced over her shoulder at the copper head tilted towards her, openly doubting the sincerity behind his comment. Again she examined the strong character lines of his face, handsome and powerful, reckless and ruthless, and very compelling.

'I don't need your pity,' she retorted waspishly, refusing his sympathy.

Fire flashed momentarily in his expression, then Barrett averted his head, reaching into his pocket to remove a piece of paper and pen. Suspiciously Dani watched him write on the paper and hand it to her.

'Here's the telephone number at my apartment,' he said.

Dani stared at it, making no move to take the paper. 'Why would I want that?'

'If you run into any difficulties in the next couple of days, I'd like you to feel free to call me,' Barrett replied patiently.

'I won't need your phone number because I won't require your help. I'm not a child. I can handle anything that comes along,' she told him sharply.

'The way you handled the reporters?' he mocked softly.

'I know you believe you rescued me, but I could have got away without your help,' Dani snapped. 'I appreciate the lift, but my friend is waiting for me.'

'Yes, I'd forgotten about your friend.' Open doubt and amusement was written on his face.

Dani tossed a last poisonous glance at him before she shoved open the door and stepped on to the concrete sidewalk. As she slammed the door shut, she heard her name called. Her head jerked in surprise, then a triumphant smile lit her face as she saw Manny Herrera walking quickly towards her. She knew very well that Barrett King would assume she had intended to meet Manny, and she purposely struck up a conversation with the jockey while the sports car pulled away from the kerb.

The instant the cream car was out of sight, she excused herself and hurried into the café, going directly to the enclosed public telephone booth where she dialled the number Marshall Thompsen had given her.

Always impulsive as she was, it never crossed Dani's mind that a more cautious person would have thought twice before contacting a virtual stranger. Her father had pushed her out on her own, extracting a promise that she wouldn't revert to the world of horse-racing which was the only life she knew. She had never had any interest outside horses. At this point she was open to any suggestion.

Marshall's assertion that he could make her a model was an intriguing one, especially if there were no strings attached. His additional statement that Barrett King might not like what he had in mind only added to her curiosity. Whether she was attractive enough or had the figure to become a model, Dani had no way of knowing, but she had picked up the confidence in the columnist's tone. Besides, he looked like a man who knew what he was talking about. And Dani was confident that she would be able to tell whether his proposal was sincere or if he was only trying to take advantage of her.

Half an hour after she had called him, Marshall Thompsen walked into the café, his dark gaze sweeping the clean but uninspiring interior with a disdainful eye. Last night he had taken her by surprise, only allowing her time to form a hasty opinion. As he slid into the booth seat opposite her, she began a discreet study of him.

Living around a race track all her life, Dani had

learned to spot the difference between the professional gambler and the average man, a wealthy person from a well-dressed person, a confidence man and an honest man. Rarely was she ever wrong.

Marshall Thompsen was dark and handsome. That much she remembered from last night. Now she noticed the softness in his chin and jaw, the slightly petulant pout of his lower lip, not altogether unattractive, yet she knew he couldn't compare with the strength in the lines of Barrett King's face. The even tan she suspected came from a sun lamp, while she was positive Barrett's was the result of many hours spent in the outdoors. Nor was there the suggestion of muscular hardness beneath the well-tailored jacket.

In a Thoroughbred, these faults would have disqualified him as good material because it would reveal he lacked stamina and heart. With humans, Dani had learned that you had to be more broad-minded. So the faults she noted were balanced by the intelligence of the wide forehead and the sharply observant dark eyes. She tried to guess his age and decided Marshall must be a couple of years younger than Barrett King, which would put him in his very late twenties or very early thirties.

As the waitress placed Marshall's requested cup of coffee on the table, Dani decided that as long as their relationship was based on business she could trust him.

'I wondered if you would call me this morning.' He glanced at her briefly as he stirred sugar into his coffee. 'Somehow I felt sure you would.'

'You made certain of it by keeping your proposal very mysterious,' Dani guessed accurately.

'It pays to not reveal your cards all at once,' Marshall smiled. 'If you were the faint-hearted type, frightened by your own shadow, you wouldn't have been of any use to me and you wouldn't have phoned me. Now I know that if you agree to my offer, you'll be capable of carrying it out.'

'Exactly what is your offer?' She forced him to meet her gaze. 'You said last night you could make me a model. How would you go about doing that?'

'First I would take you to a hair-stylist and see what could be done about that virtual crew-cut you wear, then some respectable clothes. There's a certain professional photographer who owes me a favour. I wouldn't presume to promise that I'll make you a top-flight model. Being photogenic doesn't open the door to success.'

'However?' Dani prompted, knowing there was something more behind his offer.

His smile broadened at her failure to be swept along by his offer. 'As I said, I'm a columnist with a fairly well-known reputation in certain social circles. The power of the printed word could make you fairly well-known in a short time, a minor celebrity you might say, enhanced by the fact that you've already received considerable publicity. I could be a Professor Higgins to your Eliza.'

Dani clasped her hands around the coffee cup in front of her, her nails bluntly short but curved and rounded. Her hands were slightly calloused from grooming and saddling horses, carrying water buckets and hay, and mucking out stalls. The idea that she could resemble the glamorous women she had seen in magazines was amusing. Marshall had indicated that he would be Professor Higgins, cultivating her into becoming a lady. There was a wry twist to her mouth as she thought what she really needed was a fairy godmother with a magic wand.

A sensible voice inside questioned her half-formed agreement to his proposal. But there were two things that provided a formidable agument—her own discovery last night that beneath her ill-fitting clothes was an attractive figure and her father's statement that she didn't know what it was to be a woman, let alone a lady. If there was only the slimmest chance that Marshall could succeed, Dani knew she had to take it. Not for the money or the possible success as a model, but for her father.

Yet she wasn't prepared to voice her agreement so quickly. Her impulsiveness was now tempered with caution. There were a few more things she wanted to find out.

'Suppose you do a bit of doctoring with clothes, a new hairstyle and make-up, and your photographer friend does agree that I have possibilities, what then?' Dani challenged.

'I'll see to it that you're invited to all the parties attended by the right people. Who knows? You may be able to snare yourself a wealthy husband,' Marshall shrugged. 'It's really up to you.'

'I'm not interested in men.' She dismissed the thought as unworthy of discussion.

'Men will be interested in you,' he said dryly.

But Dani had already pushed the idea to the back of her mind. 'What are you going to get out of all of this? What's in it for you?'

'Didn't your papa ever teach you not to look a gift horse in the mouth?' he mocked.

'He may have done, but at the price of grain these days, you soon realise that you never get something for nothing,' she countered.

'Would you believe me if I said it was merely an act of kindness?' Marshall asked lightly. Dark brows raised over his equally dark eyes in an expression of pseudo-innocence.

'No.' There was a suggestion of a smile in the up-turned corners of her mouth.

'I thought not,' he murmured with a soft chuckle. 'You and I are going to get along very well, I think. Your candour is very refreshing. It's rare to find a female who prefers plain speaking to feminine deception.'

'Which still isn't an answer to my question.'

'No, it isn't.' There was a significant pause as Marshall hesitated before making a further reply. 'Perhaps I only want certain people to see that things are not always what they appear to be.'

'Would one of those people be Barrett King?' Dani suggested.

'It could be.' Marshall smiled and pushed his cup away from him. 'Well, what's your answer? Are you game to give it a try?'

'Yes,' she said firmly without any qualifications or explanations.

'Then let's be on our way. We have a great deal to do and little time to accomplish it.'

CHAPTER FOUR

A HALF an hour later, Marshall parked his car in front of an elegantly imposing one-storey building, bearing the name 'Giorgio's'. Nothing on the outside indicated the type of business within, but Dani guessed it was expensive.

As Marshall escorted her inside, she knew her conclusions had been correct when she spied the imported crystal chandelier in the waiting area and the pastel blue carpet with the dainty Victorian chairs in matching blue velvet. But it took her several seconds to realise that she was in a beauty salon. The beautifully coiffed woman who came to greet them glanced rather contemptuously at Dani and with an obvious question at the darkly handsome man accompanying her, showing her sincere doubt that they had come to the right place.

'I'm Marshall Thompsen. Giorgio is expecting me,' Marshall announced.

The name Giorgio worked its magic and the woman immediately smiled. 'Of course, Mr Thompsen. This way, please.'

Without another glance in Dani's direction, she led them down a carpeted hallway, rapped lightly on a door, opening it only after a voice inside had replied. Announcing that Mr Thompsen had arrived, the woman smiled again at Marshall and started back to the reception area. A hand on her elbow firmly pushed Dani inside the room.

'Hello, George,' Marshall greeted the man who turned at their entrance.

Giorgio, or George as Marshall had called him, was of medium height and slender build. His dark hair was winged with silver-grey. There was a suggestion of Italian descent in his sharp profile and in the bright, appraising dark eyes that turned their gaze on Dani.

'Hello, Marshall. When you spoke of bringing me a challenge, you didn't add that it bordered on an impossibility. Is it a boy or a girl?'

'May I present Miss Danielle Williams? Danielle, this is Giorgio Caprio, a valued confidant of mine and a master stylist.' The introduction was made with exaggerated formality.

But before Dani could make a suitable reply, Giorgio had nodded and said, 'Of course, it is a girl. The boys wear their hair much longer.'

Without wasting any more time in idle conversation, Giorgio took her hand and led her to the large chair in front of a lighter mirror and a counter with its multitude of bottles and hair rollers. He ran his fingers experimentally through her short brown hair, checking its length and fullness.

'What crime did you commit, Miss Williams,' he demanded, 'to prompt someone to chop your hair in such a barbarous fashion?'

Under his critical and criticising eye, Dani found she was embarrassed by her appearance, something that had never troubled her greatly in the past. A pale pink stain coloured her cheeks.

'I did it myself,' she admitted in a low, apologetic voice. 'It was easy to take care of this way.'

She wished Giorgio would have erupted in a violent scolding rather than stare at her in a silent and effective reproval. Through his eyes, she could see how uncomplimentary the side part was and the way she had combed her hair behind her ears. It took all her willpower not to attempt to sink into the cushions of the blue chair.

'While you work your magic,' Marshall spoke up, 'I'll see about some clothes.'

'Earth tones and simple lines. No ruffles or frilly stuff,' Giorgio stated firmly.

'Ahh,' it was a soft sighing sound of triumph from the young columnist. 'Then you do agree Danielle is far from hopeless.'

But the look the stylist shot over Dani's head plainly said he would voice no such admission, and she swallowed nervously as the door closed behind Marshall. She sat patiently while Giorgio brushed, combed, and arranged her hair in various ways, remaining silent until she saw the scissors in his hand.

'You aren't going to cut it?' she protested in a surprised voice, then added in a quieter tone in case he thought she was trying to tell him what to do, 'You did say it was too short already.'

'It is too short,' he admitted sharply even as the snip of the scissors sounded near the back of her head. 'But it needs shaping. Since I cannot make your hair longer, I must do what I can with the little you have. Is that all right?' The last was added with deliberate sarcasm.

Firmly reminded that he was the expert and not she, Dani lapsed into silence, observing his every move when she could, but never offering a comment unless asked, which was rare.

After her hair had been shaped and shampooed, the short strands were somehow twisted on tiny rollers. Then she was placed beneath a dryer where a manicurist appeared and began repairing the years of neglect to her nails and hands. When the last application of clear nail polish was applied and had dried, the hair dryer also stopped.

Instead of leading her to the chair and having the rollers removed, Giorgio took her to another smaller chair with a lighted mirror, where he gave a stern lecture on the care of her skin. Cleansing creams, astringents, moisturisers, make-up bases, blushers, eyeshadows, eye-liners, mascara, eyebrow-pencils—she was instructed in the use of them all. Then under his artful guidance, she was instructed in how to use them, always being cautioned against a heavy hand.

'Wearing too much make-up is a greater crime than wearing too little,' he reminded her impatiently for the fourth time as he made her dab away most of the blue shadow on her eyelids.

Finally he was satisfied with her efforts, but he refused to let her dawdle in front of the mirror, staring at the surprisingly attractive face that looked back. Back she was taken to the first chair where the rollers were removed and a stiff brush was raked through the short curls, almost flattening them completely.

The chair Dani sat in was turned away from the mirror so she couldn't see the results of his work as Giorgio later combed, and fluffed and flattened. Before he was finished, Marshall walked into the room, his dark eyes lighting with pleasure when he looked at her. Whatever inner apprehensions she felt fled at the reassuring admiration in his expression.

When the stylist had completed his work to his satisfaction, he started to turn Dani around, but Marshall's upraised hand halted him.

'Not yet, George. When Danielle sees herself, I want the transformation to be complete.' The barely noticed packages he had placed in the chair upon entering the room were picked up and handed to Dani. 'Change into these and promise not to look in the mirror until you're dressed,' he ordered.

Butterfly wings of excitement fluttered inside her stomach as she promised her compliance, her eyes glittering at the pleased expression on both men's faces as they left the room. Before she could give in to the almost overwhelming curiosity to see herself, Dani fervishly began untying the packages.

The contents ranged from silken undergarments to a new pair of shoes, but the antique gold trouser suit in a shimmering material was the thing that truly caught her eye. With fumbling fingers, she stripped free of the suddenly distasteful jeans and blouse and slipped eagerly into the new clothes.

When she was finally dressed, Dani was torn by uncertainty, afraid that she might be disappointed by what she saw. So instead she flung open the door and stepped into the hall. Marshall and Giorgio were a few feet away in deep conversation, but turned as one when she appeared.

'Fantastic!' Marshall breathed.

'Do I look all right?' Dani pleaded, very femininely needing more than one word to assure herself

'Do you mean you haven't looked?' The stern expression left Giorgio's face as he smiled.

'No, I thought ... maybe ...'

'Go and see for yourself,' the stylist prodded gently, turning her around and pushing her into the room. 'I've never known a beautiful female who was so unanxious to gaze at her own reflection!'

With a mixture of awe and disbelief, Dani looked at the—yes, attractive was the word- -girl in the mirror. Feather-soft waves of rich brown hair curled about her forehead and ears, accenting the perfect oval of her face and the strong cheekbones. The clinging material of the trouser top set off her slender figure, making much of the gentle swell of her breasts and her narrow waist, while the deep gold shade of darkly ripened wheat was a perfect foil for the warm darkness of her hair and eyes.

Dani frowned, as did the girl in the mirror. 'It doesn't really seem like me.'

'You'd better get used to that image,' Marshall chided, 'because the old one is gone for good. You'll never be able to revert back to your old ways without seeing yourself as you could be today.' To Giorgio, he said, 'You can throw her old clothes in the trash. She won't be needing them any more.'

'No!' Dani protested as she stepped quickly towards the small pile of clothes, knowing the money was still in the pockets of her jeans. 'I . . . I want to keep them!'

'Nonsense!' Marshall retorted sharply. 'You have no need for those rags.'

'I want to keep them,' she asserted more firmly, quite prepared to do battle to enforce her statement.

'Let her keep them,' Giorgio inserted gently. 'They would be an excellent reminder to keep her head from becoming too big for her brain.'

'Very well, Marshall gave in, however ungraciously. 'Put them in one of those boxes and take them out to the car. I'll be with you shortly.'

Dani did as she was told before Marshall changed his mind and hurried to the car, missing the startled glance of the receptionist that quickly turned to one of amazement. A satisfied smile was on Marshall's face when he slid behind the wheel a few minutes later.

'I knew I was right about your potential, he commented as the car pulled out of the parking kerb on to the street. 'But I truly didn't expect George would be able to make such a startling change. I'm going to have to revise my schedule.'

'Your schedule? For what?' Dani queried.

'For your unveiling,' Marshall replied complacently. 'Which reminds me, I've made an appointment for you with George this Saturday morning.'

'So soon?'

'Yes, so soon,' he chuckled.

Dani leaned back against the plush cushions of the car in a thoughtful silence, realising her carefree attitude towards her appearance was at an end.

'Tell me, Marshall, how did you become friends with a man such as Giorgio? I mean ... he doesn't strike me as the type you would associate with,' silently reminded of the touch of snobbery that surrounded Marshall.

'My dear girl,' he laughed, 'more secrets are revealed in a beauty salon than in any other place. George passes any relevant information on to me. In return, I occasionally mention his establishment in my column. To borrow an old cliché, he scratches my back and I scratch his. The same goes for the shop where I got the outfit you're wearing and all the other clothes I had sent to your apartment.'

64

'You mean you didn't pay for this?' Dani gasped, fingering the gold top in surprise.

'In this case, because I needed an entire wardrobe, there was money involved, but only a fraction of the cost,' he admitted. 'Don't worry, Danielle. When you begin earning money, I'll present an itemised account of the money I've invested in you.'

'You said something about my apartment?'

'You do need some place to stay. There was a vacancy in the complex where I live, so I made arrangements to lease it.' His sideways glance glittered laughingly over her. 'Your apartment is a considerable distance from mine.'

'Will you be doing the landlord a favour, too?' Dani mocked cynically.

'Unfortunately not. This complex happens to be the exclusive kind that doesn't like publicity,' Marshall sighed with pseudo-regret.

'What happens if none of this turns out the way you planned? You're expending time and effort and money on me with no guarantee that I'll be able to pay you back,' she asked, secure in the knowledge she had the money should he demand repayment.

'You aren't very trusting,' he teased.

'Considering the types I've met around the race-track, I've learned that not everyone has a heart of gold.' Her mind instantly thought of Barrett King, a man she wouldn't trust any farther than she could throw him.

'In the first place, my plan will work. But if, as you

say, it failed, I hope I would realise it was bad judgment on my part and be content to cut my losses. I promise you, Danielle,' he said with obvious laughter in his voice, 'I won't sell you to the white slavers to recover my investment. I told you there would be no strings attached. The gamble is mine and the loss will be mine, if there is any. Does that satisfy you?'

'Yes,' Dani nodded, adding with an impish twinkle, 'so long as you remember if your plan does fail.'

'We're going to get along very well, I think,' Marshall smiled.

'Where to now?'

With the last of her doubts set aside, Dani was quite eager to step into this new existence, chasing away the nagging pain that her life would be quite different if The Rogue were still alive. She refused to admit that she was missing the bustling activity around the stables at this time of the morning. This was her father's wish and she couldn't let him down.

'To the photographer's first,' Marshall was answering, 'then somewhere for lunch.'

During the next few days, Dani felt as if she had been caught in a whirlwind. The constant activity made the loss of The Rogue easier to tolerate and the emptiness of being away from her father less consuming. Still there were times when she wished for a familiar face, even that of Barrett King's that could link her new life with the old. Every minute of her days was organised by Marshall with tours of local art galleries, sessions with the photographer, posture les-

66

sons to add grace to her already supple body, and instruction in wines and foods to enable her to choose intelligently from the menus of the finest restaurants.

Even her so-called idle hours were controlled. The music on the record player was supplied by Marshall to teach her an appreciation of classical music. Reading, too, was from books that he deemed necessary to improve her cultural background.

At nights, Dani tumbled into her luxurious queen-size bed exhausted, too weary to ponder about the abrupt about-face her life had taken. In spite of her excessive tiredness, she couldn't break the habit of rising with the sun. It was in the mornings when she wished for the sweet smell of hay and the impatient whickering of horses to hurry with their grain. Many contented hours she had spent rhythmically running a curry-comb over sleek, shining coats. Yet through all her wistfulness of those uncomplicated days ran the painful memory of the last morning she had spent at the track and the fateful breakdown of The Rogue on the home-stretch.

Before the anguish of that moment overwhelmed her, Dani would recall the last visit of her father and the real reason why she was here in this empty apartment. And whatever plans Marshall had made for the day, she would throw herself in with them, driven by an even sterner resolve to succeed and become the sophisticated lady her father wanted.

As she emerged from the taxi returning her from her Saturday appointment with Giorgio, Dani saw

Marshall's car parked in front of her apartment. With a sigh of regret for the loss of a precious free hour that she had saved strictly for herself, she hurried into the two-storey Colonial brick building and to the door where Marshall stood impatiently waiting.

'You're early,' she accused, removing the key from her purse and unlocking the door. 'Where are we off to this time?'

'Absolutely nowhere,' he replied, as he followed her into the apartment.

Darting him a disbelieving look, Dani wondered if she was in for another session of current events and sincerely hoped not because she didn't feel up to it.

'I stopped by to tell you that John was called out of town this morning and your session with him has been cancelled for this afternoon.' John Henning was the photographer, a man not easily impressed or as confident as Marshall that Dani could have a career as a model although he was willing enough giving her a trial and never sounded displeased with the results. 'And'—Marshall went on, the pause attaching importance to his next words,—'to help you pick out what you're going to wear to your unveiling tonight.'

'Unveiling?' Dani stopped in the centre of the living room and gave the tall dark man her complete attention.

'Yes, I've taken the liberty of accepting an invitation on our behalf to attend a small party being given tonight by the Whitney Blakes.'

'This is it, then,' she murmured. 'The first real test.'

He must have caught the slight note of apprehension in her voice because his smile was deliberately meant to instil confidence. 'Don't worry. You'll come through with flying colours.'

As Dani finished dressing that evening and nervously adjusted the long folds of her skirt, she couldn't convince herself it would be as easy as Marshall had indicated. Once she had believed that people of Barrett King's type were no better than she, but that was before the full extent of her ignorance had been drummed into her head this last week.

Fingering the large topaz pendant that matched the stones dangling from her ears, she meticulously scrutinised her appearance, needlessly straightening the waistband of the gold, brown and white plaid skirt. The chocolate brown knit top with cutaway sleeves and a turtle neck artfully set off the topaz necklace. The sophisticated young woman in the mirror was still a stranger to Dani, but she had to admit she could find no fault with her, except that there might be too much apprehension in the hazel eyes.

Marshall arrived promptly at seven and with his flair for idle conversation managed to push the upcoming party aside while they dined at a local restaurant. Not until they were nearly at their destination did he speak of the evening ahead.

'Are you nervous?' he asked gently.

'A little,' Dani admitted, breathing in deeply, grateful for the dimness of the car which concealed the tightness of her smile.

'You'll do fine,' Marshall assured her. 'There are only a few things for you to remember. Don't try to show your knowledge. At best, it's only superficial right now. If you don't know what someone is talking about, admit it. However, if you are asked your opinion about something you do know, give it frankly and honestly. Don't worry if it contradicts the opinions of others. Attractive women can be found anywhere, but a woman with candour is rare.'

'I hope I don't let you down,' she murmured, her eyes widening as Marshall turned into the long driveway leading to an elegant white mansion.

'You won't let me down because you won't let yourself down. You're not that kind of girl,' he answered shrewdly, slowing the car to a stop near the entrance as a uniformed attendant sprang forward to open the doors.

For over an hour they, as Marshall put it, circulated, eavesdropping on conversations that ranged from gossip to horse-racing to political policies. Sometimes they paused with a group, Marshall always instantly recognised and included while he carefully drew Dani into the conversation, bolstering her confidence until she finally relaxed.

A lively debate was going on in the mixed group next to them and Marshall steered her towards them. They stood ignored on the fringe for a few minutes, during which Dani was able to grasp that they were discussing the merits of a certain book.

'Marshall, you're just the man to settle this,' one of

the more ardent spokesmen declared as he spied the dark-haired man to his right.

'Settle what?' Marshall asked dryly, tucking his hand securely under Dani's elbows so that as he was drawn into the group, she came with him.

'What's your opinion of Hugo Freeman's latest book *The Power*?' asked a woman in gaudy jewelled glasses, rapidly losing the fight to remain middle-aged.

'I'm afraid I haven't had time to read it,' he apologised with an uplifted gesture of his hand, then he glanced speculatively at Dani. 'But I believe I saw you reading it the other day, Danielle. What did you think of it?'

She smothered a smile. He knew very well she had read it. It was one of the books he had insisted that she read.

'Yes, I did try to read it,' she said calmly, addressing her reply to the woman, determined to heed Marshall's advice to answer honestly. 'I spent half the night with the dictionary on my lap trying to decipher what I was reading. I finally ended up reading the dictionary. It was much more interesting.'

A stunned silence followed her words. A red stain began to mount in Dani's neck as she began to think she had said something unforgivably stupid. Then the man who had drawn Marshall into the conversation began to laugh until tears ran from his eyes.

As he attempted to wipe them from his face, he turned to the woman who still retained a look of hauteur. 'When you ask for an opinion, Katherine, you'd better be prepared for it to be different from your own. Marshall, I insist that you introduce me to this attractive and witty young lady. She's truly a breath of fresh air in the stagnant atmosphere.'

Marshall made the introductions around the small group, but in the wave of names, Dani only recalled those of Katherine Alberts, who grudgingly smiled after her reprimand from the man called Dru Carmichael.

There was a brief but good-natured discussion concerning the verbosity of that particular author. Then Dru Carmichael turned to Dani, a bright twinkle in his blue eyes.

'Have you read *The Love God*?' he asked

There was no mistaking the rosy flush that coloured Dani's face as she remembered the graphically lewd novel. 'The last time I saw such language written down, I was in the public rest-room at the race-track.' Her tone of voice was laced with disgust and distaste.

'Hear! Hear!' Katherine Alberts applauded.

But Dru Carmichael ignored the endorsement. 'The race-track? Is that where I've seen you before? There's something about you that's vaguely familiar.'

'There was a write-up in the newspaper about Miss Williams recently,' Marshall replied with deliberate casualness. 'And her horse, The Rogue.'

'With Barrett, of course!' The man snapped his fingers as if switching on a light in his mind. 'You're that young girl who collapsed in his arms. I stand corrected, young woman, although you certainly

72

didn't look it in those newspaper photographs.'

'Yes, Miss Williams is something of a dark horse.' The low, deep-timbred voice prickled the hairs on the back of Dani's neck. She turned with a start, staring into the narrowed gaze of Barrett King, her heart leaping in surprise.

'Barrett, this is a surprise,' Marshall stated. Yet Dani had the distinct impression he wasn't surprised at all. In fact she was convinced he expected Barrett. 'Sherry told me only yesterday that you were going to be spending the weekend at the farm.'

'Really?' The dry tone of Barrett's voice openly doubted the statement. The crooked smile he gave Dani didn't hide the coldness in his green eyes. 'Although I must admit to being surprised to find you here, Dani.'

'It isn't a pleasure for me either,' she retorted, tossing a resentful look at Marshall.

'I never said it wasn't a pleasure to see you,' Barrett mocked. 'In fact I was beginning to become curious about where you'd disappeared to.'

'I really don't know why you should be.' Dani stiffened instinctively, knowing how she had deliberately deceived him. 'It's none of your business where I go or what I do.'

'Please,' Marshall raised his hands in false placation. 'This is a social gathering, hardly the place for a re-enactment of one of your scenes.'

'I won't be making a scene,' Barrett said blandly, turning his head slightly to survey indifferently the dark-haired man standing beside Dani, not missing the slightly possessive hold Marshall had on her arm. 'In fact, I was about to ask Miss Williams to dance with me.'

His statement caught not only Dani off guard, but Marshall as well. She glanced at him quickly, almost beseeching him not to give his permission as she watched the hesitation in the dark eyes.

'Come now, Marshall,' Barrett chided sardonically at the continued silence. 'Surely you can see the head-lines in tomorrow's paper—"Feuding pair seen dancing cheek to cheek". Or perhaps you're trying to protect Dani because you think she's afraid of me. You're not, are you, Dani?'

'Of course not!' she answered sharply, and immed-iately knew he had backed her and Marshall into a corner.

'Then shall we dance?' Barrett enquired with an arrogantly patronising tilt of his auburn head.

The look that Marshall gave her indicated that she had no choice but to agree. Reluctantly, Dani placed her fingers in the outstretched palm, fighting the desire to pull away from the firm hold.

CHAPTER FIVE

'I DON'T want to dance with you, you know,' Dani muttered unnecessarily as Barrett weaved her in and out of the groups.

'I would never have guessed by your enthusiastic response.' Despite the dryness of his tone, his steps never faltered as he drew her nearer to the room where the music was playing.

'If you knew I didn't want to, then why did you ask?'

'All the usual reasons a man asks an attractive woman to dance.' The crooked smile deepened the lines around his mouth as the devils in his green eyes mocked her.

No suitably cutting retort sprang to her lips, so she clamped her mouth tightly shut.

The impromptu dancing area consisted of a space cleared of chairs and tables with the music furnished by an elaborate stereo system. A heavy beat tune was coming from the speakers. Dani halted at the edge, forcing Barrett to do likewise as she stared at the gyrations of the dancers, a younger group than Marshall had introduced her to so far.

'Something wrong?' Barrett queried lightly.

'Yes,' she hissed, and his copper head had to bend nearer to her mutinous expression to catch her words. 'I don't know how to dance that way.'

'That's a relief, because neither do I.' That silent

laughter was back in his gaze, but Dani had to admit it was more at the situation than at her.

She refused to be mollified by that. 'Since we aren't going to dance, you can take me back to Marshall.'

'Oh, but we are going to dance,' he assured her with a glitter.

Her hand was still firmly clasped in his as he led her away from the dance area. The house was large and guests seemed to be scattered all through it, clustered here and there in various groups. His long stride never slackened, maintaining the momentum that drew her along while he moved familiarly through the house.

'Where are we going?' she demanded, but he didn't answer.

As they turned down a corridor, the guests were left behind. Dani didn't have to be told that they had entered a private sector of the large home. Its very emptiness was explanation enough.

'We shouldn't be here,' she protested as Barrett opened a door and pulled her somewhat unwillingly into the room. 'I'm sure we aren't supposed to be in this part of the house.'

'The Blakes are my godparents. They won't mind,' Barrett shrugged, closing the door behind them and releasing Dani's hand for the first time.

Rich mahogany panelling gleamed on all sides except for one wall that was a series of shelves filled with books. The study appealed to Dani, with its homey atmosphere of leather-covered furniture and polished wood. She barely noticed Barrett walk to one polished wood table until soft music filled the room. Then her gaze spied the radio and shifted uncomfortably to the tall figure making his way across the room towards her.

'I've changed my mind,' she said through the tight lump in her throat. 'I don't want to dance with you.'

'You should have considered that possibility earlier when I first asked.' Already he was standing in front of her.

'You can't make me,' Dani asserted, cocking her head in a defiant angle.

'You think not?' Barrett replied quietly, too quietly, turning his words into an unspoken threat.

If Dani had missed the warning, his level gaze was daring her to challenge him. She was instantly reminded of the newspaper photograph that had shown him carrying her so effortlessly in his arms and knew the expensive material of his jacket sleeves concealed a muscular strength superior to hers. And she knew beyond a doubt that he wouldn't think twice about using it.

With an exaggerated show of reluctance, she placed her hand in his and suffered the firmness of his arm around her waist, staring at the buttons on his shirt rather than at the triumphant gleam in his eyes.

For several minutes she remained stiff and unyielding in his arms until the soothing music began to ease the tension and strain that had subtly become a part of her because of the strangeness of her surroundings and new life. Inches in front of her was the hard muscular wall she had tried to batter down, but it wasn't the anger driving her fists against it that she remembered. It was the comfort and warm support that had closed around her when a pair of arms had drawn her against that chest. Gradually, without conscious direction, Dani allowed herself to become pliant in his arm.

As the last notes of the song faded away, a reluctant sigh slipped from her throat while she drew her arm down to press a hand against his chest and push herself away. As her head raised, a tender, probing kiss caressed her lips, like summer lightning, white-hot and fleeting with its warmth.

Her eyes widened accusingly. 'What did you do that for?'

'To say thank you for the dance, of course,' he replied smoothly. 'Does a kiss have to have some special meaning?'

'No,' Dani said hesitatingly, trying to guess what was going on behind that complacent exterior and failing.

'You did tell me you'd been kissed before,' Barrett reminded her. 'I didn't think that little peck would offend you.'

'It didn't offend me.' Which was strangely the truth. She wouldn't admit that she had found it disturbingly pleasant. 'It surprised me, that's all.'

'The next time I kiss you, I'll be sure to warn you,' he stated, crooking his mouth into a half-smile as his

78

arm fell away from her waist. Before she had a chance to step in and say there wouldn't be a next time, Barrett walked away, adding almost indifferently over his shoulder, 'Are you particularly anxious to rejoin the party right now?'

'Why?' parrying his question until she discovered why he was asking.

'I don't care for parties myself. I prefer the peace and quiet of a room such as this,' he commented, settling himself into a leather chair and stretching his long legs on to the accompanying footstool. 'Do you like parties?'

'I haven't been to very many,' Dani hedged, still not totally trusting his motives.

'One isn't much different from the next.'

'If you feel that way, why did you come?' she asked curiously.

'As I said, the Blakes are my godparents. They expected me to attend and, since I didn't have any conflicting business appointments, I couldn't deliberately disappoint them,' Barrett replied evenly. 'Unless you feel you have to return to Marshall, I'd like to stay here for a little while and relax.'

Dani had no idea what Marshall expected, but the prospect of nestling in the thick cushions of the empty leather chair next to Barrett's was inviting. It had seemed a very long time since she had sat and relaxed. Always she had used any idle time to read the books Marshall had given her or listen to his records.

'I can stay for a few minutes,' she agreed, missing

the amused light that gleamed momentarily in Barrett's eyes at the qualification in her tone as she leaned back in the chair beside him.

A gentle silence rested companionably between them for a few minutes before Barrett spoke.

'When are you planning to rejoin your father?'

'Actually, I'm not,' Dani answered, turning her head in the cushion to look at him.

She had expected to see a piercing sharpness in his expression, but the lazy contentment written in the carved teak profile convinced her he was only making idle conversation.

'You knew that the day you were released from the hospital, didn't you?'

The slightly smiling look he gave her indicated that he wasn't the least bit offended that she had succeeded in fooling him. 'Yes.' Her mouth curved into a smile at her admission. 'Lew and I had talked the night before and decided to go our separate ways.'

'Your father was in favour of it?'

'Of course.' Dani stiffened, not liking the hint of reproval in his tone.

'Sorry.' There was a slight movement of his shoulders, shrugging an indifferent apology that added silently that it was none of his business. 'The few times I've seen you and your father together, you always seemed to be so close. I always admired the warm relationship the two of you had.'

His compliment washed away her momentary resentment. 'I never thought you noticed us as any more than the owners of The Rogue,' she murmured.

'Are you serious?' he chuckled softly, a pleasant sound that ran over her shoulders and down her spine. 'Do you honestly think I could forget that cheeky little brat who kept sassing me every time I came anywhere near her?'

'I do let my tongue carry me away sometimes,' Dani admitted ruefully.

'Is Marshall helping you to change all that? By the way, how did you meet him? He's not your run-of-the-mill newspaper reporter.'

She suspected something more behind his questions than simple curiosity, but in view of their previous idle conversation, she couldn't be sure.

'He saw the article in the paper and came to see me at the hospital,' she answered. The truth was always the best. 'It was after Lew and I had our talk and Marshall offered to help me find a job.'

'So he's the one I have to thank for your transformation from a child to a woman.' His gaze slid over her in silent appraisal. 'I suppose he's responsible for the clothes and the hairdo, isn't he?'

Dani didn't miss the underlying note of disapproval. 'I'm going to pay him back. I already have a job.' She didn't add that it was temporary or that John Henning had taken her on as a model with the proviso that if she didn't work out she was out of a job, and with little chance of getting another one.

'As a model, of course.'

'Why do you assume that?' she demanded.

'That's Marshall's type.'

'Why? Simply because he likes his women to be beautiful and sophisticated? The same could be said for you, Mr King. I've seen some of the women you've had hanging on your arm.' Her temperature was up.

'I don't expect a woman to be perfect,' Barrett offered dryly.

'Neither does Marshall!'

'Then why has he already changed you to fit his standards?'

'That's an absurd argument!' Dani protested. 'Before tonight would you have considered asking me to dance?'

'No,' Barrett admitted with a twinkle in his eyes. 'But I also considered myself old enough to be your father.'

'You knew that morning in the hospital how old I was, and you still didn't consider me worthy of your attention,' she reminded him waspishly.

'As I recall, I waited around so I could be on hand to rescue you from the clutches of those reporters.' The lines deepened around his mouth.

'That may be so,' Dani acknowledged grudgingly, 'but it was still Marshall who recognised the fact that I was an attractive woman and not a cheeky brat. And he is also the one who was interested enough to do something about it!'

'That's what is important to you, isn't it?' There was a fractional narrowing of his gaze. 'Before tonight, I saw you as a long-legged filly just beginning to shed her winter coat. A bit high-strung and fractious with certain people like myself, but with a big heart, always ready with a smile or an encouraging word. The winter coat is gone. But the sleek, shining coat that should be there is covered by artificial trappings and finery that detract from the inner beauty. I much preferred the old Dani to the one sitting beside me.'

Her mouth opened and refused to close as she bounded to her feet, incapable of believing that he actually meant what he said.

'I'm curious, Dani, what you hope to gain from this peacock existence. I wouldn't have thought money was important to you,' Barrett mused.

'It isn't!' she protested vigorously.

'Then what is your goal?' Slowly and casually, Barrett straightened to his feet, towering over her like an inquisitor. 'Do you want to be the darling of the social set? Spend the rest of your life parading around on Marshall's elbow to spout your cute little opinions? He'd like that. Oh, I'll admit your outlook is refreshing, as Dru said, and no doubt you spoke the truth, but is that all you want out of life—to be attractive and good newspaper copy?'

'How dare you?' Dani spluttered.

'You always gave me the impression that you enjoyed working with horses,' he went on, 'that you were content with the life you and your father led. Why this abrupt departure? I can't believe it was The Rogue's death that brought it about. You've been raised around horses and racing. The unexpected is always expected—you know that.' The questions, the subtle accusations, rained upon her head, delivered by a quietly aloof voice.

'Do you want to know why?' Dani was angry now. 'I'll tell you why! And it was because of The Rogue! Do you know what my father told me at the hospital? That he should have sold The Rogue to you, not because he was eventually destroyed. Oh, no, Lew wasn't trying to wish a mishap on you,' she jeered. 'He believed he should have sold The Rogue to you because he didn't deserve to own a horse as good as The Rogue.'

The slight jerk of his chin indicated that the words came as a surprise to Barrett.

'And the unbridled way I attacked you made him decide that he was a failure as a parent, too. He wanted me to become a lady, and that's exactly what I'm going to do!' Dani finished.

She spun on her heel and would have stalked from the room if a hand hadn't pulled her up short and pivoted her sharply around.

'Wearing expensive clothes and jewellery, being able to discuss the latest literature or opera season, and being invited to exclusive parties doesn't make you a lady, Dani,' Barrett told her sternly. 'The qualities you're looking for, Marshall will never be able to teach you.'

'How do you know?' she demanded sarcastically.

'Because he isn't a gentleman.'

'Neither are you!' she retorted. 'You're just an

arrogant, hard, unfeeling monster who doesn't like it when people get the better of him. For some reason, you resent the fact that Marshall is helping me and you're trying to turn me against him.'

'You don't know very much about Marshall Thompsen,' he said grimly.

The tautness of his jawline, the unshielded fire in his eyes, the impression of muscles tensed to spring were all danger signals warning her of her impudence. A wise person would have taken note of them.

But Dani felt no caution. 'I bet you can hardly wait to enlighten me about Marshall!' hurling her angry words at him.

Lean fingers closed over her bare arms, tightening when she tried to pull free. Then her blazing eyes watched the magical transformation as the grim line of his mouth relaxed into a coaxing smile and the leaping flames in his eyes changed into lights of beguiling imps, a witching transition that caught at her breath and reminded her sharply of his virility.

'Look, I don't want to quarrel with you,' Barrett murmured. His low-pitched, husky voice felt almost like a physical caress. 'Why can't we carry on a civil conversation?'

'Because I don't like, and you can save your famous King charm for someone else.' Not for the world would she admit that it had any effect on her.

'You obviously like and respect Marshall. I shouldn't have tried to force my opinion on you. A person should defend their friends.'

'You don't mean that,' Dani accused. 'You're only saying that because you think it might make me like you.'

'Maybe I just don't want you to dislike me so much,' he suggested, bending his head and brushing her lips lightly with his own, igniting that pleasant, shooting fire again that disturbed her senses.

'Why did you do that?' she protested angrily, although her voice wavered, taking out most of the sting.

'Because I like to,' Barrett replied with barely concealed amusement.

'Well, don't do it any more.'

'Why? Don't you like it?'

Barrett was obviously teasing her now and Dani found it was very difficult to remain angry, a discovery that endeared him to her.

'No, I don't think I do,' was her prim answer as she sought to put him in his place.

The warmth of his hands left her shoulders and her skin shivered at the unexpected removal. The fact that she enjoyed his touch she dismissed as ridiculous.

'As long as there's room for uncertainty, there's always the hope that we can become bitter friends instead of bitter enemies,' he murmured.

'Marshall must be wondering where I am,' Dani remarked sharply, prepared to do battle if Barrett suggested that they remain longer in the study. The atmosphere in the room had become too intimate for her peace of mind.

But Barrett put forth no such argument, only gestured mockingly with an outstretched hand for her to precede him to the door. Determined to keep her footsteps unhurried and not reveal to him how anxious she was to escape his presence, Dani was unconscious of the regal tilt to her head as she walked at his side, the dignified carriage of her head accented by the high turtle-neck top of chocolate brown. The style intensified the slender length of her throat and the feathery soft waves of her gleaming brown hair. As they walked down the corridor towards the chattering noises of the party, she felt his gaze straying to her and sensed the glimmer of amusement in the clear depths of his eyes. Her chin tilted higher.

'I suppose you would be annoyed if I asked to see you again,' Barrett said blandly. His offhand manner irritated her.

'Probably,' Dani agreed, arching a brown brow as she sent him a cool glance to show the last thing she was interested in was his company.

'Well, I'm asking.' There was that deep smile that managed to mock and be devastatingly attractive at the same time.

'You're right—I am annoyed.' Dani averted her gaze, letting it flit over the crowds as if she were seeking Marshall when in truth the only person she was truly conscious of was at her side.

'Is that a yes or a no?' he asked with maddening persistence.

She stopped and squared around to face him. Her

pulse quickened as she met his steady gaze. 'Why would you want to see me? You've already made it clear that you object to the way I am now.'

'I like the old irascible Dani who always manages to surface when I'm around. I don't want her to disappear completely amidst all the finery,' Barrett replied easily, then shrugged. 'Of course, if you think Marshall will object to my seeing you——'

Breathing in deeply, Dani remembered the implication from Marshall that he and Barrett might be enemies, and Barrett's reaction tonight had seemed to enforce that. She didn't think to remind herself that she had considered Barrett an enemy, too. At the moment he represented a link with the past. She had only to close her eyes to visualise him standing in front of the racing stables talking to a jockey or a trainer while examining a fleet-limbed Thoroughbred. Despite her promise to her father, she was reluctant to sever this last link with the world she had loved.

'I doubt if Marshall would approve,' she admitted hesitantly.

'I wouldn't want to put you in a position to contradict his orders.' His solemn expression didn't convey the mockery she thought she had detected in his voice.

'Marshall is helping me.' Her voice placed emphasis on the word 'helping'. 'He doesn't control my life. What I do with my free time is my business,' she asserted, her independent nature resisting any implication that someone other than herself was dictating her wishes.

'Then perhaps you'll consent to spending some of your free time in my company?' Barrett prompted.

'Perhaps,' Dani conceded. Her heart gave a strange leap of gladness as she made the tentative agreement and she turned quickly away in case that inner excitement was revealed in her face.

'Where are you staying?' His hand was touching her elbow, prompting her into resuming their way through the crowd.

'The Kingswood Arms,' keeping her voice calm and controlled. 'It's an apartment complex——'

'Yes, I know where it is,' Barrett assured her. 'There's Marshall. He doesn't look too happy. I must have kept you too long.'

Dani spied the dark face glowering at them a few feet away. Suddenly she realised that she didn't want an argument springing up between the two men. If they were ever at loggerheads, she would have to take Marshall's side, and she didn't want to align herself against Barrett. That knowledge was a surprise and one she didn't want to examine too closely.

With a nervous smile, she turned to Barrett. 'I want to thank you for the dance. I ... I enjoyed it.' Her smooth statement faltered a little towards the end.

'You want to say your goodbyes now and avoid a confrontation, is that it?' His head tilted sideways in a confiding manner, the dark auburn hair catching the fire of a chandelier and reflecting a shimmering copper hue.

Her mouth opened for a split second in surprise at

his astuteness. 'A confrontation?' she parried lamely, wondering if he could read her mind.

'Never mind,' Barrett grinned. 'I'm going to look up our hosts to say goodbye, then I'll leave. But I'll be seeing you'—a finger traced the delicate line of her jaw to her chin and lightly touched her lips— 'soon.'

After sketching a mocking salute in Marshall's direction, Barrett winked at Dani and withdrew into the crowd. A part of her wanted to watch the compelling figure until it was out of sight, but she firmly shook the desire away and crossed the short space to Marshall's side.

'You certainly took your time about coming back!' he nearly snarled.

'I didn't know I was supposed to be gone only a set number of minutes,' Dani retorted, assuming again the regal angle of her chin.

'I never dreamed you would find Barrett King's company so enjoyable that you'd have to tear yourself away from him,' Marshall jeered.

'Spare me your sarcasm!' Fire flashed in her hazel eyes. 'You knew all along that Barrett was going to be at this party and you didn't see fit to tell me.'

'There was a distinct possibility that he wouldn't be here,' he hedged, glancing around as if he expected someone to be listening. 'I suppose he filled your head with dire warnings about me.'

'As a matter of fact, he didn't,' she answered sharply —a half-truth, since Barrett had only implied that

Marshall was not to be trusted.

There was open disbelief in the dark coals of his eyes as he studied her expression, then a complacent smile turned up the corners of his mouth, the blackness of his eyes taking on a triumphant glitter.

'I imagine he was too busy gloating over the latest victory of that horse he owns, the one your horse beat the other day.'

'Easy Doesit?' Dani murmured, pain flicking lash-sharp over her at the vision of the flashy gold chestnut galloping down the straight and the even more poignant image of The Rogue.

'I guess that's the one,' Marshall shrugged, as if the subject was of supreme indifference to him.

'No.' Her head moved slowly from side to side, a puzzled frown creasing her forehead. 'No, he didn't mention it to me.'

'All that's behind you, anyway,' he said with a consoling smile, tucking her hand beneath his arm. 'Come on, there are some people I want you to meet.'

Meekly Dani submitted to his guidance. The news of the Thoroughbred's victory came as a surprise—more so because Marshall had been the one to tell her, as if he wanted to open up old wounds. But she didn't begrudge the chestnut its victory. In a way, she was almost glad. After all, The Rogue had beaten him soundly.

It was difficult to concentrate on the group of people Marshall introduced to her because her mind kept wandering back to Barrett. Why hadn't he told her?

CHAPTER SIX

THE sun had been up a long time before Dani drowsily blinked her eyes open. She rolled over wearily and glanced at the clock on the bedside table. Ten o'clock. Stifling a yawn, she slid from beneath the covers and shrugged into a light cotton robe before making her way to the small kitchen in her apartment. After filling the electric percolator with coffee and water, she padded into the bathroom where she sluiced cold water on her sleep-encrusted face. The make-up bottles and tubes were in an orderly row in front of her.

'Uggh!' Dani shuddered expressively as she glared at them.

She hadn't returned from the party at the Blakes' until the wee small hours of the morning—this morning it was. No wonder she had slept so late! With a grimace of resignation, she touched some mascara to the tips of her lashes and applied a bit of pink lipstick after brushing her teeth and ignored all the bases and blushers and coversticks.

'Marshall told me to relax today,' she murmured to herself, and stuck out her tongue at the bottles. 'I don't feel like being a glamorous model today!'

Sifting through the clothes in her closet, she chose the most casual of her outfits, white slacks and a knit top of wide gold and orange stripes separated by narrow bands of white. Running a brush through her hair, she paused through habit to fluff and curl the ends the way Giorgio had taught her to achieve the desired hairstyle. She walked into the kitchen just as the coffee pot emitted its last dying sigh.

Before she could pour herself a cup, there was a knock at the door. Muttering imprecations at Marshall for arriving before she had drunk her morning coffee, Dani stalked to the door, cursing him silently again because he hadn't called to let her know he was coming. With an irritated expression on her face, she flung open the door and stared into the green eyes that glittered laughingly back.

'What are you doing here?' Dani stepped back, her heart skipping a beat in surprise.

'I came to see you.' Barrett made a mocking show of examining the number on the door. 'This is Danielle Williams' apartment, isn't it? Or have I inadvertently knocked on the door of the Wicked Witch of the West?'

An unwilling smile edged the corners of her mouth, but she refused to submit to his teasing voice completely. 'I haven't had my coffee yet this morning.'

'In that case, may I join you in a cup?' His head was tilted inquiringly as he supported himself on an arm propped against the door jamb.

'Do you think we could both fit?' she countered, the old vaudeville joke leaping forward before she could prevent it.

'Your age is showing,' Barrett laughed.

'You're welcome to a cup by yourself,' Dani grinned, turning to lead the way into the kitchen.

'Did you just get up?' he asked lightly. 'That party must have lasted half the night.'

'I think it did,' she sighed, and poured two cups to the brim. 'I hope you don't take cream, because I haven't spent enough time in the apartment to stock it properly.'

'My father taught me to drink it black. It puts hair on your chest,' Barrett mocked as he straddled a chair and took one of the cups from her hand.

'What are you doing here this morning?' she asked between sips of coffee.

'As I said, I came to see you,' he retorted with the barest glimmer of a smile.

'That's not what I mean.'

'I didn't think Marshall would have anything planned for you today, since it's the Sabbath. I thought you might be at a loose end and I could offer my company for a tour of the town.'

'I've seen enough museums and galleries and concert halls to last me for one week. Thanks, but no thanks,' Dani replied firmly.

'I was thinking of something more in the line of a steamboat trip down the Ohio River, or maybe just a stroll along the banks. I doubt if either one will do much to improve your mind.'

His suggestion was inviting. Still Dani paused. 'We'll end up arguing. We always do,' she sighed.

'I've been subject to the sharp edge of your tongue

before,' Barrett replied, concealing a smile. 'I'm willing to take my chances.'

'It will be good to be out of doors,' she agreed with a decisive nod.

'So it's not an invitation to a day with me you are accepting, but an opportunity to be outside,' he mocked.

Dani refused to be baited into admitting that the prospect of his company for the day wasn't as unpleasant as she thought it would be. It seemed her attitude towards Barrett King had undergone a change almost as startling as her appearance. Not that she trusted him, because she was certain there was a hidden motive behind his attention that she didn't know about.

'The hardest thing I've had to adjust to is being inside most of the time,' she said instead.

'And have you? Adjusted?' Indolently his gaze left the coffee cup in his hand to sweep over her face, but Dani knew that apparent laziness hid a sharp perception.

She made a pretence of draining the coffee in her cup. 'Of course,' she declared airily.

'That's good,' Barrett said, still thoughtfully studying her. 'I wouldn't like to think you were unhappy in your new life.'

'Why would you think that I would be?' Dani countered.

'A few minutes ago you were ready to turn me down when you thought I was going to take you to some museums and art galleries. You could have been getting tired of all that culture Marshall is pouring down your throat.'

'Just because you've been accustomed to beautiful clothes and fancy parties and art objects and classical music all your life there's no reason for you to make fun of me because I want to learn about them!'

'I'm not making fun of you, Dani,' he replied patiently in the face of her defiant outburst. 'In fact, I admire you for what you're doing. The point I was trying to make was that smaller doses of culture might be more beneficial. When too much time and emphasis is placed on the paintings of a master, a person can lose sight of the fact that there's as much beauty in the crayon drawing of a child.'

His profound statement left Dani momentarily speechless. She stared unblinkingly as he, in effect, dismounted from his chair and walked past her to refill his cup from the pot. There was a fleeting sense of irritation at the way he was making himself at home before Dani sprang to her feet to face him.

'I don't believe you!' Her arms were rigidly extended at her side, her hands clenched into tight fists. 'You aren't the kind of man to know about things like that!'

The sideways look he gave her was half cold, half puzzled. 'Why not?'

'Oh, you always say all the right things, but it's only an act with you!' she declared. 'It's sickening the way people always hurry around to admire you. It always made me boiling mad the way Lew would proudly answer any patronising question you asked!'

The kitchen was small and little distance separated them. In the flickering of an eyelash, Barrett reached out with a long arm and took hold of her wrist. She was jerked forward within inches of his ruthlessly cold face and the taut line of his mouth.

'I never patronised your father!' he snapped, an iridescent sheen of satanic flames glittering in his eyes. 'If I ever asked for his opinion it was because I valued his answer and judgment and I asked for *only* that reason. Despite any other idiotic notions you have, your father is an excellent horseman and a fine trainer. I admire him as other men more experienced do.'

'That still didn't stop you from trying to buy the finest horse he ever owned!' Dani shot back, refusing to believe that Barrett was sincere.

'There were other offers for The Rogue besides mine, weren't there?' As her mouth clamped shut, he gave her a shake, guaranteed to rattle anyone's teeth. 'Weren't there?' he demanded again.

'Yes!' A sarcastic and reluctant admission from Dani.

'But it still sticks in your craw that I offered to buy him—no one else, only me! And it never occurred to you that you might be treating me unjustly.' The initial explosion of fire was gone, leaving a cold anger in its place. 'I should take you over my knee and paddle you the way your father should have done a long time ago.'

The threat wasn't carried out as Barrett released her wrist in disgust while the humiliating truth of his words sunk in. She hadn't treated him fairly. She might have even misjudged him, but it didn't explain why she always felt she had to be on her guard whenever he was around.

She stared at his averted head, proudly arrogant, and the slightly embittered lines around his mouth. Her honesty demanded her to make some concession to the truth, but she refused to let it be at the cost of her pride.

'You ... you might be right,' she said hesitantly. 'I may ha ... have done you an injustice.'

Barrett turned back, a cynical smile crooking the corners of his mouth, then slowly it changed into a rueful smile. 'I lost my temper, didn't I?' he sighed, the impish light returning to the green depths. 'I'll accept your apology if you accept mine.'

'It's accepted,' Dani agreed, feeling somehow the blame had been equalled.

'Have I ruined our day?' he asked quietly.

'I don't know.' A little frown wrinkled her forehead as she took his question seriously. 'It sort of cleared the air, didn't it?'

'It may have,' Barrett conceded. He held out his hand to her. 'Friends again?'

Dani smiled, 'Bitter friends,' and placed her hand in his.

'Come on, I'll buy you breakfast before we take a ride on the *Belle of Louisville*,' he offered.

After they had eaten breakfast at a small but very hospitable restaurant, Barrett and Dani strolled about the river front taking in the futuristic architecture in the seven-acre park called Riverfront Belvedere. Sometimes they talked. Sometimes they walked in silence, gazing at the flowers and shrubs or the fountains and reflecting pools that abounded. The latter, Barrett informed her, were used for ice skating in the winter.

The park was guarded by a statue of George Rogers Clark, the founder of Louisville. But the star of the park was the Ohio River, broad and somnolent, flowing ever onward.

Then came the trip on the *Belle of Louisville*, a triple-decked sternwheeler. After touring the first two decks, including the sweeping ballroom, Barrett took Dani to the open-air deck on top where a calliope was all steamed up and its brass whistles were blowing a lively tune. As the *Belle* manoeuvred away from its wharf into the river channel, the couple moved to a vantage point at the railings.

'Has she always been here?' Dani asked, watching other tourists and sightseers waving to the boat from the shore.

'No, she started out as a ferryboat and packet on the Mississippi River out of Memphis, Tennessee, but her home is here in Kentucky now,' Barrett replied. 'Kentucky could be technically considered one of the thirteen colonies, since most of the State was once a part of Virginia.'

'I thought this afternoon wasn't supposed to improve my mind,' she teased with an impish grin.

'I decided you should have some trivial information at your fingertips in case the conversation ever gets boring at one of the parties,' he chuckled in return.

As they watched the slowly changing scenery before them, there was no strident demand for conversation as Dani had experienced at the party the night before when she had been with Marshall. The silence was as comfortable and reassuring as the hand that rested lightly on her shoulder. However, the thought of the party and Marshall did arouse the need to have her curiosity of the night before satisfied.

Switching her gaze from the water being churned up by the paddlewheel to the strong features of the man beside her, Dani asked, 'Why didn't you tell me about Easy Doesit winning the race yesterday?'

'How could I have done it without dredging up more painful memories for you?' His level gaze held hers, stating a fact without offering any sympathy.

'That's true,' she admitted, the slight pucker of a frown above the bridge of her nose as she looked towards the distant banks. 'I'm not ... I mean, I don't mind your horse winning.'

'I'm glad to hear that,' was his reply, then he tactfully steered the conversation away from horses to point out a particular landmark that was coming up.

As far as Dani was concerned the trip ended all too soon. She was enjoying the breeze that ruffled her hair, the sun beating down on her face, and she was enjoying the company of the man beside her. Her footsteps dragged a bit en route from the dock to the parking lot where Barrett had left his sports car.

'Are you hungry?' he asked as he slid behind the wheel of the car beside her.

'Yes.' A hopeful light shone in her eyes that maybe he wouldn't take her immediately back to that empty apartment.

'Good. We'll go get us something to eat,' Barrett nodded briskly as he put the car in gear and reversed into the traffic.

Ruefully Dani glanced down at her simple slacks and top. 'I'm not dressed for it, I'm afraid.' A wistful sigh slipped from her lips.

'You look fine to me, and the place I have in mind won't have any objections to the way you're dressed. Marshall can take you to the posh restaurants in town.' There was a mocking glint in the glance he gave her. 'I'd like you to sample some of our local fare.'

The moment Dani stepped inside the restaurant, the cheery atmosphere seemed to say welcome. Its whole decor was homespun and bright with an abundance of yellow and greens. There was little resemblance to the elegant establishments that she frequented with Marshall, places where she was always terrified she was going to use the wrong silverware.

'This is nice,' she murmured as she sat in the chair Barrett held for her.

'Don't sound so surprised,' he laughed softly, taking a chair on the opposite side of the table. 'Didn't you think there were any other decent restaurants other than the ones Marshall chose?'

'Of course, it's just——'

'I know, you like it.' The teasing smile took her off the defensive and drew an answering smile. 'The specialities of the house are burgoo and hot brown.'

'What are those?' Her eyes widened with laugher at the strange-sounding names.

'Hot brown is a sandwich of turkey, bacon and cheese topped with a white sauce. It's very delicious and a local favourite,' Barrett explained. 'Burgoo is probably a dish of the first settlers in Kentucky. It's a peppery hot chowder of beef, ham, chicken, and vegetables.'

'I like anything hot,' she admitted. 'I'll have the burgoo.'

'Wise choice. I think I'll have the same.' He gave the waitress their order when she arrived, then turned to Dani. 'Well? Did you enjoy the trip?'

'Oh, yes,' she responded eagerly. 'And the walk along the riverfront, too.'

The bubbling but subdued happiness subsided as she saw Barrett glance at his watch. Was he regretting asking her to eat with him? Maybe there was somewhere else he had to be?

'Six hours without an argument. That must be a record.' She drew an almost visible sigh of relief at the teasing expression on his face. 'Why do you suppose that is?' he asked.

'Maybe because you've stopped treating me like a child,' she returned lightly.

'I don't see you as a child any more.'

The husky, enigmatic tone of his voice reached out to touch her, as did the caressing look in his eyes. That old tingling sensation raced down the back of her neck, only this time it wasn't born of antagonism, but something else that Dani couldn't put her finger on. It somehow made her disturbingly conscious of him as a man, a compellingly handsome and masculine individual and not a tenuous link with the world she missed.

Fortunately their food arrived just then and she was able to shake away the uncomfortable wanderings of her thoughts to concentrate on the peppery stew. During the meal, there was little need for conversation, and afterwards, comfortably full, there was even less.

A short time later Barrett stopped the car in front of her apartment. Dani turned to thank him for the day, believing he intended to let her out as Marshall always did, only to find he was already out of the car and walking around to her side. Some of her surprise must have registered in her eyes as she stepped out of the car under his guiding hand.

'I'll see you safely to your door,' was his explanation.

In the hallway in front of her door, Dani removed her key from the slender clutch purse she carried. Barrett slipped it from her hand and inserted it in the lock before she realised what was happening. She stood hesitantly in front of the now opened door, wondering if she should invite him in.

'I . . . I had a wonderful time today,' she offered uncertainly.

'So did I.' An indefinable gentleness was in his voice as if he were attempting to soothe a high-strung colt.

'Would you like to come in for coffee?' she suggested, trying to steady the sudden increase in her heartbeat.

'I'm afraid I can't.' Barrett handed back her keys.

'Of course.' Her clipped reply was sharp as she realised how silly it was to think that Barrett might want to spend more time with her. 'Thanks again for taking me out.'

She took a hurried step into the doorway, only to have his hands close over the upper part of her arm.

'Not so fast,' he chuckled lightly, drawing her a step backward at an angle that brought her closer to him. A finger tipped her chin upwards. 'I prefer a more demonstrative thanks.'

This time when his mouth touched hers, it lingered, tenderly probing the softness of her trembling lips. The warm, persuasive kiss was oddly satisfying and totally unlike the furtive and unpractised ones Dani had received from others in the past. His lips were hard and sensual, no fleeting lightning bolt this time, only golden fires in the kiss that had no foundation in gratitude. When he slowly drew away, the firmness of his possession remained imprinted on her mouth. Dani resisted the impulse to put a finger to her lips as she gazed at him with rounded eyes.

'I'll be seeing you,' Barrett winked, and gently pushed her into the apartment and closed the door.

That indefinite promise made the evening alone seem not so long, although Dani would have vigorously denied that her thoughts ever turned to Barrett King except to dwell on some of the pleasanter aspects of the day.

Monday morning brought the return of her hectic schedule, throwing her into the tedious business of a model. She didn't mention her afternoon with Barrett to Marshall because she didn't think it was important. It certainly wasn't because she thought Marshall would object.

Monday stretched into Tuesday and Tuesday into Wednesday. The time that wasn't spent with the photographer, Marshall claimed with his unending demands to see this or read that or attend this party or that concert.

When he dropped her off at her apartment Thursday evening loaded with more books and records as well as a detailed description and review of the latest creations from Paris, Dani had to stifle the desire to dump them back on his lap. She felt too exhausted to care about her ignorance. She was so busy juggling the bundle in her arms trying to extract the key from her purse that she didn't notice the man leaning against the wall of the corridor opposite her door.

'It's about time you got home,' a low voice commented.

Dani turned so abruptly that two of the books slid from the stack on to the carpeted floor. Barrett stepped forward as she bent to retrieve them.

'I didn't mean to startle you,' he apologised.

'Well, you did,' Dani said crossly. 'You shouldn't pop out at people from the dark.'

'I thought this hallway was fairly well lit,' Barrett commented blandly, a bemused smile flitting across his strong mouth.

His accurate observation earned him an angry glare. 'What do you want?' As she straightened to her feet, the articles once again stacked in her arms and the door key in her hand, Dani noticed the large package, flat and square, in one of his hands and a paper sack in the other. A tantalising aroma drifted by her nose.

'I thought you might not feel like going out to eat tonight, so I brought the meal to you,' he said, his straight face giving way to a witching smile. 'I hope you like pizza, because this is too big for me to eat by myself.'

Whether it was the appeal of his smile or the hunger-evoking scent coming from the box, Dani's initial irritation began to recede.

'I like pizza,' she admitted, inserting the key in the lock and turning it. 'But how do you know that I'm not going out to dinner?'

'I checked my sister's calendar. I didn't see anything on it that would warrant Marshall's interest, so I took the chance that you would be free,' Barrett replied as he followed her in, a somewhat sardonic gleam in the green eyes. 'From the looks of you, you needed the night off.'

Setting the books and records on the coffee table in the living room, Dani sighed a little dispiritedly. 'I don't have the strength or energy to debate the point,' she explained, turning around to follow Barrett, who was already depositing his packages on the kitchen table. 'Let me do that,' she said as he began unloading the groceries from the sack.

Instead of stepping aside, Barrett took her by the shoulders, turned her around and pointed her in the opposite direction. 'You can go take a shower and relax. I'll put the pizza in the oven to keep it warm and toss together a salad.'

'You?' Dani said in disbelief, looking over her shoulder, his hands preventing her from turning around. Barrett simply didn't seem the domesticated type.

'Who did you expect? My chef and valet have the night off, so that only leaves me.' he mocked, giving her a little push to send her on her way. 'And hurry up, because I'm hungry!'

The spray of the shower was relaxing, rinsing away the tension that had knotted her muscles. If it hadn't been for Barrett's admonition to hurry, Dani could have remained a long time under the stinging spray. But she turned off the water and briskly rubbed herself dry, then slipped into the long terry robe. As Dani stepped into the small hallway en route to her bedroom, Barrett's voice called out to her.

'It's about time! I was beginning to think you'd been washed down the drain.' Then he added, 'The food is on the table.'

'I'll be there in a minute,' she promised gaily. 'I have to get dressed yet.'

He stepped into the archway of the hall, the overhead light touching off red fires in his dark auburn hair. 'You look substantially clothed to me. Come on, let's eat!'

Dani glanced down at the white wrap-around robe. It certainly covered everything there was to cover from her ankles to her neck with only a very discreet vee to expose the hollow of her throat. With a shrug to herself that said, 'Why not?' she changed her direction and walked down the hallway to the kitchen.

Two bowls of lettuce salad were on the table, the chunked green leaves mixed with cherry tomatoes, carrot shavings, green peppers, onions and topped with an anchovy. Dani slid quickly into the chair Barrett held for her, finding that she too felt ravenous. The salad was soon disposed of and Barrett placed the pizza that had been kept warm in the oven on to the table.

'And I was going to settle for a bowl of soup tonight,' she sighed, appreciatively inhaling the spicy tomato sauce mixed with peperoni and sausage and cheese atop the crust.

'All food tastes good when you can share it with someone,' he commented as he handed her a wedge.

'Providing the company is right,' Dani added before she bit into the pizza.

'I hope you're implying it is,' he smiled.

'I wouldn't dream of insulting the chef,' she teased. 'He might serve me poison the next time!'

Their light-hearted banter continued through the meal, remarkably free of any hostility or any thought of hostility. If Dani had been amazed when Barrett shooed her out of the kitchen to cook the meal, she was doubly amazed when he helped with the clearing up. She couldn't resist commenting on it as they made their way into the living room.

'Don't you think a man should help in the kitchen?' he countered her question.

'Well, yes, of course,' she faltered. 'But not many men would agree with you.'

'I'm not many men,' he shrugged, and walked over to the stereo set to sift through the records leaving Dani to wholeheartedly agree, though silently, that he was certainly unique and not at all like the men she knew. 'You have some pretty heavy albums here,' Barrett interrupted her thoughts.

'They're Marshall's,' she explained self-consciously, 'he likes me to listen to them when I'm not doing anything.'

'When is that?' he mocked with a wry grin, reminding her of his statement the previous Sunday that culture should be taken in small doses to be appreciated.

'Not often,' Dani admitted, sitting on the couch and curling her feet beneath her.

Barrett selected a record and placed it on the turntable, then walked over to occupy the opposite end of the couch. Leaning back against the cushions, he started to prop his feet on the coffee table, then stopped.

'Is that forbidden?' he asked with a laughingly arched brow.

'I do it all the time whether it's ladylike or not,' Dani shrugged.

'I like to stretch out.' And he slid a magazine over so his shoes would not scar the table.

Dani snuggled deeper in her corner into a more comfortable position and listened to the softly lilting melodies from the stereo, a little surprised that Barrett had chosen one of her favourite albums until she considered the fact that he seemed instinctively to know what she liked.

She had barely settled in when the telephone rang. Unfortunately the phone was on the end table on the opposite side of the couch where Barrett was seated. Reluctantly Dani untwined her legs and hopped to her feet. As she reached the spot where Barrett's legs were sprawled in her path, she noticed him reach over and remove the receiver from the hook to hand it to her.

'Hello?' She perched on the edge of the couch beside Barrett, the coiled line of the receiver crossing over him.

'Yes, Danielle. Marshall here.'

She made a face at the telephone unconsciously. 'Yes, Marshall.' A hesitant glance at Barrett caught him looking at her with undisguised interest and amusement.

'I was calling to let you know our luncheon date tomorrow will be at twelve-thirty. That will give you plenty of time to change at John's before I pick you up.'

'That's good,' she nodded unnecessarily. 'Is there anything else?'

'No, no, that's all.' There was a slight pause before he continued, 'Is there anything wrong, Danielle?'

'What do you mean?' Dani nibbled at her lower lip, anxious for the conversation to be at an end.

'You sound preoccupied. Aren't you feeling well?'

'I'm fine. I was . . . er . . . just in the middle of one of the books you gave me,' she lied, glancing at the undoubtedly mocking expression in the green eyes watching her. She shifted uncomfortably to escape the suddenly burning warmth of Barrett's thigh against hers and nearly succeeded in pulling the telephone off the table. The firm touch of Barrett's hand guided her back.

'I see,' Marshall replied, obviously placated by her statement. 'I'll see you tomorrow.'

'Yes, tomorrow. Goodbye.' After his answering goodbye, there was a click of the receiver on the opposite end and Dani breathed deeply in relief before reaching across Barrett to replace the telephone. 'Marshall was calling about an appointment tomorrow,' she said, stricken by an uncontrollable need to explain why he had called.

'That's nice.' One corner of Barrett's mouth was tugged upwards in a hesitant, crooked smile. 'Why didn't you mention that I was here?'

'It didn't seem necessary,' Dani hedged, not entirely sure of the answer herself.

'What would you have done if he'd asked you what you were reading?'

Fire flashed in her eyes for a moment before she succumbed to the laughter that bubbled in her throat. 'I have no idea!' she giggled.

When the laughter died, she found she was leaning against the back of the couch within the circle of Barrett's arms. Her still smiling face was turned up to him when she became conscious of her position.

'Stay here,' Barrett ordered gently, holding her tighter when she would have moved away.

For a moment she resisted, then allowed her head to be nestled against his shoulder. With a small sigh of compliance, she relaxed, the soothing strains from the stereo washing over her while she was enveloped in the warmth emanating from Barrett. It felt so right to be leaning against him.

CHAPTER SEVEN

'I THINK it's past your bedtime,' Barrett spoke from somewhere near her ear.

Her lashes opened slowly, weighted by the drugged half-sleep that possessed her. She gave a little sigh of contentment as she drew the arm around her waist into a tighter hold.

'I was only resting my eyes,' she claimed in defence, but her voice was soft and whispery.

His quiet chuckle was muffled by the closeness of his mouth to her hair and the warmth of his breath was like the caress of a butterfly. Beneath her head she could hear the reassuring steady beat of his heart.

'You've been doing such a good job of resting your eyes that you haven't heard a word I've said for the last fifteen minutes.' His feet were off the coffee table and back on the floor as he began to straighten. 'It's time I let you get to bed.'

'Don't go,' Dani protested drowsily, not wanting to lose the comfortable pillow beneath her head, nor the warm blanket of his arms.

But her husky plea didn't halt his movements. 'You're out on your feet, girl,' Barrett said firmly.

She felt an arm slide under her knees and in the next instant she was being carried in his arms like a child. There was no desire to protest this time as she twined her arms about his neck. The dreamlike state of half-sleep sensed the rightness of his action. Through half-closed lashes, she peered at the powerful line of his jaw and chin and the grooves beside his mouth that lessened the fierceness. As her eyes swung lazily to the thick lashes accenting the brilliant green depths of his, she found him gazing down at her, something very caressive in the look.

'I was eight years old the last time my father carried me to bed,' she murmured in a sleep-thickened voice.

He made no comment to that remark as he entered the darkened room, but Dani had expected none. Tugging back the covers of the bed, Barrett laid her gently on the exposed sheet. Her hands remained locked around his neck, holding him above her.

'Good night, Dani,' he said again in that firm voice that still sounded gentle.

'I'm still not that tired,' she said with one final protest.

In the light streaming in from the bedroom door, she saw the quirk of his mouth into a faintly amused grin. 'Of course not,' Barrett agreed mockingly. When he began to lower his head towards her, Dani tilted her chin, anticipating his kiss.

At the light touch of his mouth, a flooding warmth spread through her with the lethargic heat of an open fireplace. Her lips moved in response to his kiss, a primitive instinct telling her what to do. Abstractedly her hands felt the tightening of the muscles in Barrett's neck and the pressure of his hands at her side as he started to draw away. Under the gentle insistence of her lips, his kiss hardened into something more than a simple caress. Dani felt the stamp of possession in the sensual pressure of his mouth, arousing strange new desires, but the languorous weakness that spread through her body eliminated any attempt to resist.

Then his fingers were closing over her wrists, dragging her hands away from his neck If she had been more alert, she would have noticed his uneven breathing. Her body cried for an unknown fulfilment it hadn't received and she murmured an incoherent sound of protest.

'You're half asleep and you don't know what you're doing,' Barrett declared huskily, a trace of temper in the steel of his voice.

It was true, Dani still did feel half drugged, but whether from the exhaustion of the day or the intoxicating touch of his lips, she couldn't say.

'Go to sleep,' he ordered crisply. She felt the indifferent brush of his mouth across the top of her forehead before he pushed himself away and rose to his feet.

Her head turned against the pillow, trying to find the warmth and comfort she had known in his arms. Through heavy lashes, she watched the tall silhouette walking closer to the open door.

'Barrett,' she murmured softly, and he stopped in the doorway, the light from the hall illuminating his face as he half turned in answer. Vaguely she realised again how devastatingly attractive he could be to some women. 'Why do you suppose I don't like you?' she asked.

There was an upward tilt of one side of his mouth as if he found her question secretly amusing. 'You'll have to come up with that answer yourself, kid.'

'I'm not a kid,' she retorted instinctively.

'Good night, Dani. Pleasant dreams '

'Good night,' she echoed softly, her eyelids already fluttering down so that she didn't even see the door close.

In the next couple of weeks, Barrett came round several times, his arrival always unexpected and co-inciding with her free evenings. Sometimes he brought food to be cooked at her apartment and other times he took her out to eat. There was a friendly rapport between them, even when they argued, and her hazy recollection of their intimacy the other evening be-came something she had imagined.

Dani never mentioned Barrett's visits to Marshall. He would have scoffed at the fragile threads of friend-ship she felt towards Barrett. And she knew he wouldn't understand her desire to keep some active link with her past. A man as suave and urbane as Mar-shall would never be able to understand the earthy simplicity and satisfaction she had known. He would abhor the smell of horses and hay that clung to skin and clothes. To Dani, it was as fragrant as the most expensive perfume.

Which wasn't to say she didn't enjoy being a sophisticated young lady, or the compliments and admiring looks she received. Her reflection in the mirror no longer surprised her. In fact, she had come to expect the attractive young woman in the mirror. Subconsciously she knew the giant step she had taken into the feminine world was irreversible. Never again could she be casual about her appearance or her clothes.

She was an amazing contradiction, she decided, enjoying her new-found womanhood while preferring the simpler pleasures of her past to the hectic social whirl Marshall kept her in. Privately she was beginning to agree with Barrett that one party was not much different from another.

Marshall was in his element at the social functions they attended, handing out false compliments with a sincerity that Dani often marvelled at, her own honesty shunning such aberrations. Recognising the insincerity that abounded enabled her to keep her feet firmly on the ground when men would try to sweep her off them with extravagant statements.

Perhaps, she thought, that was another reason why she enjoyed Barrett's company. Except for an occasional comment that he liked her outfit, he never plied her with compliments. Although her earlier antagonism towards him had disappeared, she still recognised that streak of ruthlessness in Barrett, a dogged determination to get what he wanted regardless of who or what was in his way. Her antagonism might be gone, but Dani didn't believe she liked him. There were moments when his level gaze would rest on her and she would feel the prickles of unease that indicated that she still didn't trust him although she was never entirely certain why.

Oh well, she sighed aloud, it didn't really matter. Bitter friends they might be, but it was better than being bitter enemies.

'Are you tired?' Barrett asked, taking his eyes from the road illuminated by the car's headlights to glance at Dani.

'Mmm, yes,' she admitted, pulling herself out of the reverie that had held her.

'I thought for a moment you'd fallen asleep.'

'You shouldn't have fed me such a big meal,' she scolded mockingly. 'That always makes a person tired. Will you come in for coffee tonight?'

Her question coincided with the turn into the parking lot of her apartment complex. Barrett didn't answer immediately as he manoeuvred the car into a vacant spot and shut off the motor.

'Are you sure you wouldn't rather tumble right into bed?' he asked. 'I know you've had a full day.'

'One cup of coffee and then I'll shoo you out,' Dani smiled.

'That's a bargain.' He was out of the car and walking around to her side. She handed him the key to her apartment, as had become their custom, before she lightly placed her hand on his arm to walk by his side.

After opening the door, he passed the key back to her as she flicked on the light switch. 'Make yourself comfortable while I put the coffee on,' she said over her shoulder, taking three steps into the living room en route to the kitchen before she stopped short. 'What are you doing here?'

Simultaneously Dani had seen the lamp was lit in the living room and Marshall sitting with crossed arms in the chair beside it. His expression was far from pleasant as he spied Barrett standing behind her.

'I called your apartment and when I didn't receive any response, I came over to see if anything was wrong,' he answered sharply, but there was a black, accusing light in his eyes.

'As you can see, nothing is wrong,' she said, arching in defence. 'Barrett took me out to dinner, that's all'

'Oh, Barrett did, did he?' His malevolent glance swept contemptuously over the supremely calm countenance of the tall, auburn-haired man. 'How cosy!'

'That doesn't explain how you got in here,' Dani reminded him sharply.

For all her outward show of defiant composure, she was a trembling mass of apprehension inside, wondering when the whole situation was going to blow up in her face now that Marshall had found out she was seeing Barrett and hadn't told him.

'A spare key, my love,' he answered sarcastically, dangling it from his fingers. 'I must have neglected to give it to you.'

'Well, you can give it to me now!' Angrily she stalked to the chair and snatched the key from his unresisting fingers.

'You could have always had another one made for Barrett to use,' Marshall suggested.

'Dani and I were going to have some coffee. Why don't you stay for a cup, Marshall?' said Barrett, the cold gleam meeting the leashed fury of the other man's gaze.

Dani stared at him in disbelief. Here she was trying to think of ways to get rid of Marshall, and Barrett was inviting him to stay!'

'A marvellous suggestion,' Marshall agreed, rising to his feet. 'I'm surprised I didn't think of it.'

'Dani looks on you as a friend,' Barrett shrugged negligently. 'Since Dani is a friend of mine, I suppose in a roundabout way we have something in common.'

'Don't I have some say in all this?' Dani demanded angrily. 'This is my apartment!'

The level gaze swung from Marshall to her. 'Of course, you can make the coffee,' Barrett said smoothly, 'while Marshall and I decide which one of us will be the host.'

'Neither of you will be the host!' she inserted. The whole thing was threatening to get out of hand. 'You will both be my guests and you will both conduct yourselves like gentlemen.'

'Which means, Marshall, that we can trade insults but not blows,' Barrett said, his mouth moving into a humourless smile.

Dani was confused by Barrett's strange behaviour but she could tell that Marshall was even more bewildered. Barrett, who had once before eluded a confrontation with Marshall, now seemed to be inviting it. Dani glared at both men, then stalked into the kitchen to fix the coffee.

Her own temper was evidenced by the slamming of doors and clattering of cups on saucers. Yet none of the noise she made was loud enough to drown out the voices of the men in the other room, especially Marshall's, which had grown loud and rather belligerent.

'How long have you been seeing Danielle?' he was demanding.

'Several weeks now.' Barrett's voice was quieter and she found herself straining to hear it. 'Only on the nights when you weren't parading her off to your friends.'

'I always knew you had a guilty conscience about that horse of hers,' Marshall sneered

'Nothing of the sort. The girl is in a strange world. I thought she might like a familiar shoulder to lean on once in a while.'

'Familiar?' A jeering tone. 'I was the one who was there to help her when she needed someone after her father turned her out, not you. She rejected your offer of help out of hand!'

'Simply because she didn't trust me,' Barrett replied calmly.

'Does she trust you now?'

'Not yet.'

Dani's mouth opened a little, wondering how Barrett could possibly know that.

'She never will,' Marshall was saying. 'You will

always be the one she will subconsciously associate with the death of her horse and the breakdown of her father. You will be the one she'll blame for her father's failure. After all, you're Barrett King, the epitome of everything her father wasn't.'

'Surely that's to your advantage.' There was a tinge of mockery to Barrett's husky voice as if indicating that Marshall would need all the advantages he could get.

'You bet it is,' Marshall snarled. 'I made her what she is and she knows it!'

'The only thing you did, Marshall, was show her how to dress and order from a fancy menu,' Barrett said dryly. 'Dani is what she is because of her own individual personality and because of the way she was raised. All those years she spent with her father, exposed to the seamier side of life, yet she has never been tainted by any of it. I believe her father deserves the credit for that, not you.'

'I have a good mind to see to it that Danielle never sees you again,' Marshall threatened.

'And how would you go about doing that?'

'Simply remind her of the fact that she's breaking her promise to her father.' Dani's heart dipped to her shoes at the unmistakable triumph in Marshall's voice and her own slight bending of the promise she had made her father.

'How could seeing me break a promise she made to Lew to become a lady?' There was open scepticism in Barrett's tone.

With squared shoulders and a proud tilt to her head, Dani stepped into the living room. 'I can answer that question, Barrett,' she said, avoiding the piercingly thoughtful green gaze that swung on her. 'If you two will come into the kitchen, the coffee is ready.'

There was a smugly mocking gleam in Marshall's dark eyes as he took the chair directly opposite Barrett, leaving Dani no choice except to take the chair that placed her in between. Cradling her hands around the cup, she stared into the brown-black liquid.

'I promised my father,' she began slowly, 'that I would break my association with the track and that I would never have anything to do with horses or racing.'

'I don't believe your father would disapprove of you seeing me.' The quiet conviction in Barrett's voice was oddly reassuring.

'Oh, really?' Marshall jeered, 'Is that why you've deputised yourself as the official big brother to Danielle?'

Dani looked up in time to catch the look Barrett flashed across the table and shuddered at the thought if that quelling look was ever turned on her.

'I don't intend to let you have a free hand with her, Thompsen.'

'Are you worried that I'll ask her to "be nice" to someone?' the darker man returned sarcastically.

Barrett leaned back in his chair, subtly relaxing and seemingly taking command as he regarded Marshall through lazy, half-closed eyes. 'To be truthful, I almost believed that you'd asked Dani to "be nice" to me until she failed to mention that I was here one night when you called.'

A flush crept into Dani's cheeks when Marshall darted an angry glance at her. 'This whole conversation is pointless,' she insisted defensively.

'Hardly pointless,' Marshall scoffed. His darkly handsome face was now indelibly stamped with blatant sarcasm. 'Any minute now Barrett is going to relate to you a sordid tale about an innocent little girl named Melissa and how I nearly succeeded in leading her astray.'

'Melissa?' she echoed, glancing hesitatingly from one man to the other.

'The daughter of a friend of mine,' Barrett explained.

'Well? Go on,' Dani insisted as Barrett made a show of drinking his coffee as though the explanation he made was sufficient.

But Marshall wasn't going to leave it at that. 'A few years ago, little Melissa won a local beauty contest. She was engaged to be married at the time, but the bright lights and glitter suddenly beckoned her. She came to me and persuaded me to help her become a model. Of course, the version she gave her family and fiancé was that I'd approached her with promises of a great future. She was about your age and the apple of her father's eye. Anything his little girl wanted, she got, so naturally he gave his consent. The fiancé was a few years older and he wanted to give his love a chance to have fun before she settled down to married life. He consented, too.'

Out of the corner of her eye, Dani glanced at Barrett, calmly listening to a tale with an indifference that bordered on boredom. Yet she didn't think it would take too much intelligence to realise that Barrett had been the fiancé of this Melissa. The discovery brought a coldness to her chest that she didn't understand.

'The girl was beautiful,' Marshall went on. 'Unfortunately she had no desire to work. All she wanted was the prestige and excitement of being a model without the work you know it entails, Danielle. She wanted instant success, push a button and be on the cover of *Vogue*. But Melissa did enjoy the parties and the men that would crowd around her. Somewhere along the line, she took on a lover.' A derisive glance was tossed at Barrett. 'Or more than one. I have no idea whether she did it to further her career the easy way or if it was just for kicks. Either way, her fiancé found out. And precious little Melissa told him that I had asked her to "be nice" to the man. Therefore I became the villain.'

Dani's eyes were clouded with tears for the anguish Barrett must have gone through. Now she understood the animosity that existed between the two men and Marshall's cryptic statement that he wanted to show 'certain people' that things were not always what they seemed.

'The engagement was broken, needless to say, because Melissa didn't want to give up her new life.

Daddy sent her off to New York where he bought her parts in some Broadway shows and a few television commercials. I understand she's doing quite well, but then she was always a pretty good actress.'

'You neglected to mention the way you successfully turned the scandal to your advantage,' Barrett commented with marked disinterest. 'But you always were adept at using people and situations, as you've used Dani.'

'The law of survival, my boy,' Marshall chuckled smugly. 'Not everyone is born with a silver spoon in their mouth.'

'It's unfortunate that not everyone is born with compassion in their hearts for a fellow human being,' was Barrett's dry reply.

'*Noblesse oblige*, huh?' But Dani could see Marshall was faltering a little despite his continuing sarcasm under the pinning gaze of the man opposite him.

'Look, Thompsen, I may have misjudged you regarding Melissa, but I haven't made any mistake about you as a man. You're too filled with your own sense of power to spare a thought about anyone else except how they can help you.' There was something very threatening in the softly spoken words. 'Now, if you've finished your coffee, I suggest that you leave.'

Hesitation was in the flickering gleam of Marshall's dark eyes as he debated within himself whether to dispute Barrett's right to order him to leave, but Dani had no doubt that Barrett would carry through the order.

'I'll see you to the door, Marshall,' she said, pushing her chair back to rise and forcing him to accompany her.

She could feel the rage still seething in him as Marshall walked rapidly to the door, his back rigid with anger and his face black with malice. His mouth curved into a sneer as he turned to bid her goodnight.

'So you've decided to go over to King's side, have you?'

'I'm not on anyone's side,' Dani said firmly. 'I didn't want the two of you arguing any more, and this seemed the best way to stop it.'

'Don't get any ideas that his attentions towards you mean anything special. His concern comes from a stupid sense of responsibility, nothing more.' His voice and his expression were telling her she would be a fool to read more into Barrett's attentions than that. 'Let him worry about your moral character and I'll see to it that you become a success.'

'Goodnight, Marshall.'

There was a bad taste in Dani's mouth as she closed the door on the stiffly retreating figure and retraced her steps to the kitchen and Barrett.

He was no longer at the table, but leaning against the counter, a fresh cup of coffee in his hands. He didn't look up when Dani walked in.

'Barrett?' At his name, she was swept by a coolly aloof gaze. 'I'm sorry.'

'About what?' he countered as she took hesitant steps nearer.

'Melissa,' she answered without raising her eyes to meet his. 'You were engaged to her, weren't you?'

'Yes.' His voice was completely devoid of any emotion, which only made Dani realise how very deeply he had been hurt.

'You mustn't blame Marshall too much for what happened. I mean, she must have needed the adulation of more than one person before she met him,' she ended lamely.

'You're still leaping to his defence, aren't you?' His scathing bitterness reached out to slash at her.

'I wasn't really defending him,' Dani asserted, her chin raising defensively as she met the coolness of his level gaze. 'I've always known he was only helping me because he was going to get something out of it. I've never had any illusions about that. But he wasn't to blame for what happened between you and Melissa. It would have happened anyway.'

'And?' Barrett prompted with maddening cynicism. 'Your eyes tell me there's another point you want to make.'

Dani breathed in deeply to check her temper. She knew she was receiving the backlash of his anger that he had been controlling all the time Marshall was there.

'You once told me that you preferred the old Dani to the new me. But I'm basically the same person. I am what I am and the way I am, and nice clothes don't make me any different.'

This time she didn't lower her gaze under his intimidating glare. For some reason that she couldn't explain, she wanted Barrett to understand that she wasn't like Melissa. It was important to her.

'I'm doing all this because it's what Lew wanted. It's his admiration and respect that I want. No one else's!' she added when the heavy silence threatened to stretch indefinitely. 'I want him to be happy, and if wearing expensive clothes, going to fine parties, and mixing with the right people will do it, no matter how much I'd rather be with him, I'll do it.' When Barrett still failed to comment, Dani's foot stamped the floor in frustration and inverted anger. 'And I won't have you arguing any more with Marshall and wrecking my chances to be what my father wants! Do you hear?'

Her eyes were burning with acid tears and she didn't see the corners of his mouth twitch in a revealing smile.

'Yes, I guess you're still the same cheeky little brat that you were before,' Barrett admitted, a devilish twinkle replacing the coldness in his eyes.

'Of course I am!' Dani snapped, still too angry to realise that Barrett was agreeing with her.

'I'm glad you admitted that,' he mocked.

'Admitted what?' she frowned as she studied the arrogant tilt of his head. The mist of tears clouding her eyes began to diminish.

'That you're a cheeky brat,' he answered with a complacent grin.

'I did not say that!'

'No, I said it, and you agreed with me.'

Confusion reigned as Dani tried to make the lightning adjustment from anger into teasing that Barrett had made. That intimate gleam in his eyes wasn't helping her to think straight either. She heard his soft laughter and felt his arm wind around her waist and draw her beneath his arm.

'You aren't angry with me any more?' There was uncertainty in the look she gave him, her head tilting over his upper arm so she could see his sternly handsome face.

'I never was angry with you,' he said, drawing her around in front of him so that he could better see her face as he locked his hands behind Dani to keep her there.

'I thought you were,' she said, addressing the open collar of his shirt and the dark auburn hairs that curled on his tanned chest. 'Because of the things I said about Melissa. I probably didn't have any right to say them.'

'When has that ever stopped you from speaking your mind?' he mocked. His head was lowered close to her downcast face.

Without volition her hands were resting on his shirt front, her fingers playing with the opening while she fought off the peculiar catch in her breathing at the sight of his mouth so close to her own.

'I'm sorry,' she repeated. 'I know you must have been very hurt when you found out about Melissa.'

'That's all over now,' Barrett said quietly, and something in his voice convinced her that it was so. And Dani felt exceedingly glad about it. 'At the time I did blame Marshall because I didn't want to admit that Melissa was not what I thought she was. I realised a long time ago that what you said about her earlier was true.'

'Just as you've come to discover that I'm the same cheeky brat,' Dani finished with a mock sigh to conceal her joy.

'There's something else we have to talk about, Dani,' he went on.

'What's that?'

'The promise you made your father.'

The edges of her mouth drooped. 'I've bent it a little, but I haven't ever talked to you about your horses or what's happening at the track,' she said defensively.

'Why didn't you tell me about it in the beginning?'

'I didn't think you would come to see me very much. When you did, well——' Her shoulders moved in an expressive shrug, not wanting to put into words the way she had looked forward to his visits.

'You broke your word to Lew because of me.'

'Yes.' Dani buried her chin in her chest. 'Somehow seeing you helped. It suddenly wasn't so lonely.'

'Lonely? With all those parties Marshall takes you to?' His question prodded her gently.

'They're all strangers to me, the people at the parties. I've learned all the right things to talk about, but—I know I shouldn't have broken my word.'

'I don't think Lew meant you to take it literally.'

'Oh, yes, he did,' Dani nodded.

Barrett took away one of the hands at her back and reached into a pocket. 'Read this,' he said, and handed her a letter.

The scrawling handwriting was unmistakably her father's. 'How did you get this?' she breathed.

'It's a letter your father wrote me,' Barrett answered, but Dani was already busy reading it.

The letter was short, but her father had never been one for writing. The first part thanked Barrett for coming to see him and for letting him know how she, Dani, was doing. Her eyes glittered with tears as she read the last line above her father's nearly indecipherable signature. It said: 'I'm grateful that Dani is seeing you. I don't like to think of her completely alone without anyone she knows.'

'He doesn't mind,' she whispered. 'Lew isn't upset because I've been seeing you.'

'No, he isn't,' Barrett replied solemnly.

'When did you see him?' Dani blinked back the happy tears to gaze earnestly into his face. 'Was he all right? Where is he?'

'Slow down! I can only answer one question at a time.' The smile negated the effects of his stern words. 'I saw him in New York. He's at Belmont right now and he's fine.'

'When were you there?'

'Last week. He's picked up a good-looking four-year-old gelding and the mare he kept was placed in both races that he entered her in. I think he's begun to renew his faith in himself.'

'Why didn't you tell me?' Dani murmured. 'That you'd seen him?'

'He indicated that he didn't want you to know where he was, although he never told me in so many words that I couldn't,' Barrett replied with a twinkle.

'I'm so happy!' she cried, throwing her arms around his neck and hugging him tightly. 'I've been so worried about Lew, not knowing where he was or how he was. It was awful.'

'I know, kitten.'

Her face was buried in his neck. At the caressing sound of his voice, Dani lifted it slightly, glancing at the sensuous line of his mouth now crooked in a smile. As she moved closer to it, Barrett met her halfway.

CHAPTER EIGHT

SOMETHING happened in that kiss. The wild melody of joy in Dani's heart turned into a symphony, a rising crescendo that pounded in her ears until she couldn't even hear the beat of her own heart. The touch of Barrett's mouth, at first probingly soft as always, became masterfully demanding, expertly forcing her instincts to make a response.

Her breathing was a shallow, unresisting series of sighs when the exquisitely hard pressure of his mouth left hers to explore the pulsating cord in her neck. No one had ever aroused such elemental feelings in her before.

'I believe you're beginning to like me,' Barrett murmured next to her ear.

'Onl . . . only beginning,' her shaky voice decried as if she needed to deny what was happening to her.

Her hands slithered from his neck to push weakly against his chest. An instant later Dani was sorry he had so obligingly let her go. She hadn't remembered feeling so weak at the knees since she had been thrown from a horse a few years ago. Her legs had trembled so badly when she had tried to get back in the saddle that her father had to help her mount.

The long length of his body was leaning against the counter again, his dark auburn head was thrown arrogantly back while the viridescent glow in his eyes played over her face with infuriating thoroughness. Dani knew her face was much too expressive and was revealing the clamouring emotions she couldn't control.

Hoping to divert his attention, she said, 'The next time you see my father, will you give him my love?'

'Of course,' agreed Barrett smoothly. 'Oh—before I forget,' he straightened from the counter, 'I won't be seeing you this weekend. It's my parents' anniversary this Sunday. I probably won't be back in town until the end of next week.'

'Oh,' in a very small voice as her heart took a nose-dive. Dani turned away trying to assume an air of indifference. 'I hope you have a very nice time.'

'I'm sure I will,' he said with an amused lilt in his voice. 'Will you walk me to the door?'

It was her turn to murmur, 'Of course,' while she kept a safe distance between them.

With the knowledge there would be no unexpected visit from Barrett, the following days and nights seemed unbearably monotonous. Dani kept telling herself that she only missed his easy friendship. The rather tumultuous after-effects of his kiss had merely been a reaction to the news of her father. She refused to consider that she might be physically attracted to Barrett. His fierce good looks didn't affect her at all, she kept saying, and she was immune to the devastating smile.

The feeling of monotony she was experiencing was simply because she would rather be outdoors in the sunlight instead of under the bright lights of the camera, or in the fresh evening air instead of some smoky party room where there was incessant din of noisy voices. The explanation faltered when she tried to apply it to the lonely evenings that she was free and still remained cooped up in her apartment.

Marshall never mentioned that scene at her apartment. That had surprised Dani since she had expected him to grill her about her relationship with Barrett. The only subtle change she had noticed in him was that he seemed more attentive than he had been before and more confident. Her somewhat listless agreement to any suggestion he made only brought a shrewdly satisfied gleam to his dark eyes.

That same gleam had been there this afternoon when he abruptly informed her that he was changing their plans for this evening. His announcement that they would be attending a private party instead of an exclusive supper club hadn't even raised a carefully drawn eyebrow from Dani.

As usual, she and Marshall were among the last guests to arrive at the party. She had long since ceased to be enchanted by the beautiful furnishing of their various homes she had been in or the sparkling jewellery and expensive clothes worn by the people who invariably attended these private parties.

Through her experience gained at the race-track, Dani was able to separate the welcome guests from the gate-crashers and the social climbers. And Marshall was always a welcome and much sought-after guest. Every group of people they approached stepped back to admit him into their circle.

The last group they had stopped at had made him the centre of their attention, something that Marshall's ego enjoyed and Dani was grateful for, since she wasn't in the mood to exchange bright repartees.

Pretending a polite interest in the conversation, or more correctly Marshall's monologue, she let her gaze wander idly over the room, silently wishing she was out beneath the stars. At the opposite end of the room, she caught a flash of burnished copper. Shifting her position slightly, she was able to find it again.

Her heart fluttered, skipped a beat, then hammered wildly. She only knew one person who had that particular shade of auburn hair, and that was Barrett. Unconsciously she must have stiffened, communicating her tenseness to the hand that rested possessively on her shoulders. As she became aware of Marshall turning towards her, the auburn head turned, enabling her to see the powerful profile that was unmistakably Barrett's.

'Is something wrong, Danielle?' murmured Marshall.

'No, no, nothing,' she protested too quickly as Marshall's dark eyes followed the direction of hers.

At that moment the couple who had been obscuring her view of Barrett stepped aside. Before, Dani had only been able to see him because of his superior height. Now she saw the attractive blonde clinging to his arm and a numb pain took hold of her chest.

'You seem surprised to see him here,' Marshall was saying. 'Why is that?'

'I thought he was out of town,' the truth blurted itself out before she could stop it.

'He's been back for several days,' was the mocking reply. 'Didn't you know that?'

Her pride quickly surfaced as she shrugged. 'No, why should I?' But she couldn't keep her gaze from straying back to the blonde who was so obviously receiving Barrett's complete attention. Even at this distance, Dani could recognise that warm smile and that disconcerting way he had of looking at a person as though no one else existed.

'Wondering who the blonde is?' Marshall whispered sarcastically.

'I don't remember seeing her before.' The casually worded admission came out in a tightly choked voice.

'That's Nicole Carstairs—of Carstairs Steel, the current front-runner in the race to become Mrs Barrett King.' The unmistakable pleasure he took in revealing that startling information to Dani drained the colour from her face. Information like that was Marshall's speciality. There was no doubt in her mind that he knew what he was talking about. 'You didn't actually think you were the only girl he was seeing, did you?' he jeered softly. 'I tried to tell you the other night that he was only seeing you because he felt some mis-guided sense of responsibility towards you, but you didn't believe me. Or foolishly didn't want to believe me.'

She felt sick to her stomach, torn in two by some vague feeling that Barrett had betrayed her. The desire to cover her ears and shut out the horrible things Marshall was saying was nearly too strong for her to deny, yet the poise he had instilled in her kept her motionless while inwardly she was reeling from the shock.

'I understand Miss Carstairs even spent the weekend at the farm, ostensibly one of the many friends who gathered to celebrate the Kings' anniversary. Personally I think that was a secondary motive,' Marshall remarked.

'Please,' Dani protested, 'stop talking about it! Barrett and I are friends, that's all.'

'Why are you telling me that?' A superior smile widened his mouth, taunting Dani with its smugness.

She spun quickly away from his touch, hating him for telling her something she should have guessed herself. Hadn't she always known Barrett could have any girl he wanted? Hadn't she herself called him a ladies' man?

'You'd like to leave, wouldn't you, Danielle?' he said quietly.

'Could we?' Her earnest hazel eyes turned back to him, the cinnamon pupils etched with pain.

Marshall chuckled as if his triumph was complete. 'No.' His lip curled in refusal. 'Not until we've welcomed Barrett back to Louisville.'

Her horrified gaze searched the dark face, seeking some sign that Marshall was only playing a horrid joke on her. Then Dani realised he wasn't. He fully intended to take her over to where Barrett was. In that same instant she knew Marshall had changed his plans that afternoon because he knew Barrett was going to be at this party tonight and Nicole Carstairs would be with him. This was Marshall's revenge because Dani had not told him that she had been seeing Barrett.

Short of fleeing the room, there was no hope of escape. Marshall's hand was already taking her arm, turning her back around and facing her in Barrett's direction. Her mind raced ahead, trying to discover what Marshall hoped to gain by embarrassing her in this way, even as she took the first faltering step to cross the room. Then with vivid clarity, she knew. He wanted a scene. He wanted to see her make another outraged attack against Barrett in public as she had done when The Rogue was destroyed. Not to humiliate her, but Barrett.

This knowledge gave her the strength to push back her own shattered illusion and give room to her pride. The smile she forced upon her mouth as they drew nearer looked so natural that only someone who had known her for years would see the strain at the corners and the unnatural pallor of her complexion. The glazing of pain in her eyes was practically unnoticeable as she braced herself to meet Barrett's gaze that was just swinging around to her.

The brightness of his gaze faded when he saw her. Her heart cried for her to turn away, to escape the penetrating search of those green eyes, but Dani kept her feet moving steadfastly forward.

'Barrett, I didn't know you were back!' And she wondered if the delight in her voice sounded as hollow to him as it did to her. But the slackening of Marshall's hold on her arm told her he hadn't anticipated her friendly greeting. Fooling him gave her the courage to continue. 'I could hardly believe it when I saw you across the room.'

'I told Danielle that you'd been back for several days,' Marshall inserted.

'Did you now?' There was a challenging hardness in Barrett's eyes when he turned them to Marshall, but they were levelly cool when they rested on Dani. 'It's good to see you again, Dani.' The blonde at his side moved closer, her clear blue gaze openly inspecting Dani as she tried to make it obvious that she was with Barrett. 'Nicole, I would like you to meet a friend of mine, Dani Williams,' Barrett introduced. 'Dani, Nicole Carstairs.'

Dani didn't miss his failure to identify Nicole while he had labelled her as a friend. The smile she gave the attractive blonde felt stiff as her muscles rebelled.

'How do you do, Miss Carstairs,' Dani murmured. 'That's a lovely dress you're wearing.'

A statement that was much too true, as she noticed how perfectly it matched the woman's cornflower blue eyes. The blonde made an appropriate reply, quickly turning her attention to Marshall as he was introduced.

'I do hope you enjoyed your weekend at home, Barrett,' Dani found herself saying.

'Oh, we had a wonderful party,' Nicole assured her, casting an adoring glance at Barrett. 'Of course it was strictly for family.'

Dani flinched involuntarily. If she had needed any affirmation of Marshall's statement, she didn't any more. And Barrett made no denial, his silence enforcing Nicole's claim. Yet she still sought the teak-carved face, praying for any sign that the woman was exaggerating. The expression on his face was thoughtful and curious. Her heart wept a little as she watched it change into a warm smile when he looked down at Nicole.

'Excuse us a minute, would you?' said Barrett. 'I want to see Dani for a minute.'

The cupid bow mouth pouted slightly before Nicole wrinkled her nose and smiled. 'Don't be long.'

'I won't,' Barrett promised, glancing sharply at Dani when she caught her breath in surprise, then turned to Marshall. 'Keep Nicole company, will you?'

Already Barrett was reaching for Dani's hand and she wondered if he saw the flash of anger in Marshall's eyes. As she reluctantly placed her hand in his, Dani realised how very cold she was, cold and numb. There was fear in her glance to his face, fear that his peculiar perception had guessed the pain she was feeling. But his attention was on the couple he was leading her to, and Dani eyed them hesitantly.

'Dani,' Barrett was saying, 'I want you to meet my sister Stephanie and her fiancé, Travis Blackman.'

'Dani?' His sister, a very attractive girl with long brown hair, cocked her head enquiringly, then burst into a wide smile. 'Dani—of course, you're the one Barrett has been talking about. She's every bit as beautiful as you said she was, Barrett.'

Whatever Dani had been expecting the comment to be, it hadn't been that. Maybe something relating to that embarrassing publicity about The Rogue, but certainly nothing that would imply that she had been the subject of many conversations. Despite her confusion, she managed to make a suitable reply.

'Your father is Lew Williams, isn't he?' Travis Blackman enquired, drawing Dani's bewildered glance to him. She immediately liked what she saw, a pleasant face with brown eyes and brown hair.

'Yes, that's right,' she nodded.

'He worked for my father several years ago,' he explained, 'before we sold our horses.'

'Of course Daddy and I are trying to persuade Travis that he should buy some more,' Stephanie laughed. 'From the King stables, naturally,' she added with a wink to Dani.

'You'd better be careful that Dad doesn't pass a broken-down old nag off on you,' Barrett mocked, 'like the one you're about to get yourself tied to for the rest of your life.'

Thanks to Marshall's training, Dani was able to say the right things at the right time even though she had no idea what was being said. She was too conscious of the length of Barrett's body standing next to her, the burning touch of the hand that held hers, and the unshakeable feeling that she would never again be able to look on him as a friend. A subtle change had taken place in their relationship tonight, too subtle for her to grasp immediately.

The smile, the forced laughter were becoming harder and harder to maintain. Any second she felt she would dissolve into tears. Not even when The

Rogue had been destroyed had she felt such pain. In an effort to keep her sanity, her hand unconsciously tightened on Barrett's. His head bent slightly towards her, curious, questioning eyes searching her face while one corner of his mouth tilted upwards in an enquiring smile. With the force of a physical blow, his look took her breath away.

'I have to get back to Marshall.' The nearly frantic desperation in her voice brought an immediate narrowing of his gaze.

'I think he'll survive a few more minutes without your company,' Barrett remarked cynically.

But will I? Dani wondered, her heart pounding with dread that she wouldn't be able to keep up this pretence of gaiety much longer. She averted her head from the penetrating gaze, turning a wide but trembling smile to the other couple.

'It was so nice meeting both of you.' The brightness of her voice was transparently brittle, but luckily neither his sister nor her fiancé seemed to notice as they returned the compliment. When Dani turned away, she was able to free her hand from Barrett's hold. Her eyes latched on to Marshall's dark figure some distance away as if it were a lifeline.

'What's wrong, Dani?' Barrett's voice was low, but unmistakably demanding.

'Wrong? Nothing is wrong.' Flashing him an innocent look that was edged with fear. 'I like your sister. She was very nice.'

There was no comment from Barrett and when she

darted a cautious sideways glance at him, she saw the way his mouth was clamped shut in an uncompromising line. The determined set of his jaw lent wings to her feet as she hurried to Marshall's side.

The arm that Marshall slipped around her waist was a much needed support, and for the first time in Dani's experience, she felt him brush an affectionate kiss on her cheek. As Marshall bade their goodbyes to Barrett and Nicole, Dani thought in passing how strange it was that she had always looked on Barrett's embrace as the one offering comfort and security, and here she was seeking it from Marshall. At that moment, his questionable motives for bringing her to this party mattered not at all. She was too busy clinging to Marshall to notice the fire that leaped into Barrett's eyes as Marshall guided her away.

Minutes later they were out on the entrance portico of the large home waiting for the attendant to bring Marshall's car. The fresh air was a tonic to revive Dani's numbed senses, but it also stole her defences as she leaned heavily against him.

'Now will you cut him out of your life, Danielle?' Marshall demanded softly, drawing her closer.

'Yes,' she whispered.

His hand cupped her downcast chin and raised it. The shadows concealed the expression on his darkly handsome face, but Dani was too hurt to care about anything except the solace of his arms.

'I know what I did tonight must have seemed very cruel to you,' he murmured. 'But sometimes a person does have to be cruel to be kind.'

Dani didn't attempt to elude the mouth that moved to cover hers. In fact, she welcomed it gladly, needing someone's kiss to erase the memory of Barrett's. The fleeting warmth she felt seemed to succeed in doing that.

Through the enveloping fog of pain, Dani decided she had misjudged Marshall's reasons for forcing her to meet Barrett. His motive must have been a desire that she wouldn't make a fool of herself over a man who belonged to someone else.

The following day Marshall was nearly always at her side, never allowing her to be alone, always there sending her reassuring smiles to tell her that he was the only one who truly cared. Somewhere along the line Dani decided she had misjudged him. Of course, Marshall was shrewd and his actions were somewhat calculated, but to be a success in his field, he had to be. She had always known she couldn't trust Barrett just as she had known she could trust Marshall, although she had qualified it at the time that she could trust him as long as their relationship was strictly business.

That opinion was being revised with each passing minute as one thoughtful kindness followed another. Left to make her own decision, Dani would have refused to attend the dinner and theatre that night, but Marshall had insisted. And as the evening progressed, she realised he was right. Alone in the apartment she would have brooded at the way she had been deceived by Barrett's attention. It had never been friendship he was offering—she could see that now. It was as Marshall said, Barrett had simply felt responsible for her and, though Marshall never said it, Dani realised that most of Barrett's attention had been to counteract Marshall's influence, to get back at Marshall for the imagined part he had played in Barrett's broken engagement years before.

In front of her apartment, Marshall switched off the motor, but it was Dani who made the first move that brought her into his arms, although he firmly kept her there once she was encircled in his embrace. His hands and his kisses stimulated her with their ardour until finally he drew back to trace her features gently in the dark.

'This is all my fault,' he said softly. 'I thought you would reject any overtures of friendship. You were so cynical and doubting at first that I thought I had to give you time to trust me. I never dreamed that Barrett would show up or that you would seek from him what I wanted to give you.'

A heavy sigh shuddered through her. 'The only thing I was really seeking, I think, was a link with the past. That's the only reason I ever saw him.'

Initially that had been the truth. With a twinge of pain, Dani knew it had developed into a need for companionship. If only she had told Marshall about Barrett's visits, she would never have suffered the torment she was going through now, this piercing hurt that she had been betrayed.

'Are you going to be all right?' Marshall enquired

gently, brushing her lips lightly.

'Thanks to you, I will,' she smiled, giving him back the kiss and feeling his arms tighten so her mouth would linger against his for a few seconds more.

'I'll come in for a while if you want me to,' he offered.

'I'll be fine,' Dani assured him, moving reluctantly out of his arms to her own side of the car. 'I'll see you tomorrow.'

'Not until the afternoon, I'm afraid,' he said with a regretful sigh. 'I have some work I have to do. Sleep late in the morning. I'll call John and tell him to postpone your session until next week.'

'I feel I could sleep until Christmas.' A statement that was amazingly true as a delayed exhaustion seemed to sweep over her—no doubt a reaction from the sleepless hours the night before.

After exchanging goodnights, Dani walked swiftly to the entrance of her apartment building where she turned to wave to Marshall as he drove out of the lot. As she walked down the hall to her door, the carpet muffled her footsteps so that the only sound she heard was the rustling of her long gown.

Inserting the key in the lock, she opened the door and started to close it behind her, only to have it explode out of her hand by some violent force pushing it open. Her startled gaze stared at the towering figure stepping into her apartment.

'What are you doing here?' Dani breathed, intimidated by the satanic fires blazing in the green eyes contemptuously sweeping her from head to foot.

'I wanted to talk to you,' Barrett replied in a dangerously low voice. 'And I had the strangest impression that you wouldn't agree to that.'

A muscle was jumping in his jaw and the rigidity of his stance reminded her of a jungle cat about to spring. His face was carved in lines of uncompromising harshness. Her heart was beating at a frantic pace as she weakly backed away from him.

His statement was one she couldn't deny, so she attempted to sidetrack him with the first thing that came to mind. 'I . . . I didn't s—see you outside.'

'That I can believe,' he jeered softly. 'You were much too occupied with . . . other things.'

She swallowed back the nausea that rose in her throat as she realised he must have seen her in the car with Marshall. 'Th—that's none of your affair,' she protested, her voice growing stronger. Out of the corner of her eye, she caught a glimpse of the telephone beside the couch. With quickened steps she reached it and picked up the receiver with a threatening look. 'If you don't leave, I'll call the police and have you thrown out!'

With a swiftness that she hadn't expected in a man Barrett's size, he was at her side and wrenching the black receiver from her hand. And Dani knew she hadn't underestimated the strength in his muscular chest and arms. Hadn't he more than once picked her up and carried her as if she weighed no more than a child?

'You will call no one,' he told her, his head arrogantly tilted back, 'until I find out what the hell is going on!'

'I owe you no explanations.' Her tight voice threatened to break under the strain.

'I thought you knew what kind of a man Marshall is,' not letting her escape from his penetrating gaze.

'I've always been an excellent judge of people, which is probably why I never liked you,' Dani retorted.

'What's happened to you this last week?' Barrett demanded. 'Last night at the party, you chattered away, making stupid, inane remarks while recoiling from me as if I had the plague. I did try to telephone you to let you know I was back in town, but I couldn't reach you and I was too busy to get away.'

Bitterly Dani agreed that he probably was too busy. Nicole had acted as if she expected every minute of his time, but she wasn't about to voice that opinion.

'I wouldn't have cared if you never saw me again,' she said scathingly.

'I thought we'd agreed to be friends.' His words were drawn tightly through clenched teeth, the muscle still working convulsively along his jaw.

'That was before I realised that I preferred Marshall's company to yours. He's infinitely more satisfying,' she stated with a defiant thrust of her chin.

CHAPTER NINE

'You blind, naïve little fool!'

In a lightning move that she couldn't elude, Dani was jerked against him. It was like coming in contact with a high-voltage wire, jolting her to the tips of her toes. His taut thighs burned through her gown until her legs were powerless. Beneath her hands she felt the uneven rise and fall of his chest, not much different from her own ragged breathing.

'What do you know about love? Or sex, for that matter?' Barrett snarled, the leaping flames in his eyes derisively encompassing her face.

'More than you think,' she said weakly. Her gaze was uncomfortably conscious of the ruthless line of his mouth. 'I know it takes two willing people.'

A mirthless sound of laughter came from his tanned throat. 'The first time I kissed you I knew that if you'd ever been kissed before, it wasn't by a man.'

'I've been kissed before,' Dani asserted. She tried to push herself away from his chest, only to have him draw her more firmly against the long line of his body. She was disturbingly aware that the rounded swell of her breasts was being imprinted through the silk shirt on to his skin.

'Yet you believe that a man can't force himself on you,' he jeered. A wicked light entered his eyes.

'Let me go!' Dani cried, suddenly frightened by that look.

As her hands reached up to scratch at his face, her wrists were imprisoned and twisted behind her back. Before she could kick out with her foot at his vulnerable shins, Barrett was bending her backwards so she was off balance, and any attempt to defend herself with her feet would send her sprawling on the floor.

With one hand, he held both her wrists while he viciously forced her twisting and turning head to receive his bruising kiss. His mouth smothered hers, depriving her of breath while grinding her lips against her teeth. A searing fire was coursing through her, making her doubly weak and defenceless, incapable of any kind of action to resist him while her mind reeled beneath his violent embrace.

When Barrett forsook her mouth to ravage the sensitive areas around her neck and ears, Dani gasped for breath, feeling the betraying shudder of her body beneath his expert, if savage, touch. 'No,' she moaned in a plaintive protest. Her mouth opened to repeat the cry again, only to have it die in her throat as his mouth closed over hers, taking advantage of her parted lips to the fullest.

Almost of their own volition, her tense, frightened muscles began to relax, allowing Barrett to mould her more firmly against his masculine hardness. Slowly he straightened, her wrist still imprisoned, her head still bent back so he could take his pleasure of her lips. And her lips throbbed beneath the punishing assault of his mouth, a sensual pain that shot white-hot fires through her. Nothing in her experience had prepared her for the undiluted passion of his touch.

'Do you see how easy it could be?' Barrett muttered against her mouth.

The very steadiness of his voice curbed the weakness that had made her pliant to his demands. The suddenness of her struggles succeeded in freeing one of her wrists as her head twisted away from his mouth. In the next instant she found herself prone on the couch with Barrett's weight holding her there easily, his eyes glittering dangerously at the frightened roundness of her eyes. Never in her life had Dani been so aware of the difference between a man and a woman than she was at that moment when every hard, muscular contour of his body was forcibly emphasised.

'Are you going to insist that I prove it?' The softness of his voice didn't hide the steel beneath the surface.

But Barrett didn't allow her time to answer as he lowered his head again to ravish her mouth, this time with a gentle sweet seduction that disarmed her completely, compelling her to remember that sensation of security and comfort she had first experienced in his arms, coupled with a strange conviction that this was where she belonged.

Lost in the labyrinth of her paradoxical emotions, Dani blinked in confusion when his pressing weight left her body. A thousand unanswered questions in her eyes as she stared at the erect figure standing beside her.

'Well?' Barrett challenged, his hands on his hips, that unrelenting hardness still in his expression.

'I hate you!' Her voice trembled as she tried to find the strength to move from her singularly inviting position on the couch.

A scoffing sound of amusement came from his throat. 'I've been hated before,' Barrett mocked, turning away from her.

Released from his paralysing gaze, Dani struggled upright on the cushions, stung by his indifference to her statement.

'I hate better than most people!' she retaliated in a surge of childish temper.

'Is that what you felt a moment ago? Hate?' There was something very intimate in the look that swept over her, stripping her of her protective anger and exposing the naked response of her body that she was trying so hard to deny.

'Go! Get out of here!' she demanded hoarsely, hot waves of shame filling her cheeks. 'I want nothing from you. Not your friendship or your kisses! Keep your disgusting passion for Nicole. She probably loves the caveman technique!'

'Nicole?' An eyebrow arched enquiringly, then a slow smile spread across Barrett's face and he threw back his head to laugh heartily.

'I don't see anything very funny in that,' she said crossly.

The laughter stopped, but the devastating smile remained. 'So that's what all this is about,' he murmured in satisfaction.

'I don't know what you're talking about.' Dani

turned away from his much too perceptive gaze, earnestly wishing she had never mentioned Nicole's name. It was unthinkable that she could possibly be jealous of the woman.

He reached down, taking the wrists of her tightly clenched hands and drawing her to her feet. When she attempted to pull free, he raised a placating hand.

'I made an unforgivable mistake the other night and I owe you an apology,' he told her. The mutinous expression on her face changed to one of bewilderment as she warily watched the solemnly amused face for a sign of mockery. 'I assumed that you knew that Nicole and Travis Blackman, my sister's fiancé, are half-brother and sister.'

A frown puckered her forehead, afraid to believe the implication of his statement that for Barrett, Nicole didn't exist except as the half-sister of his future brother-in-law.

'Have you been listening to Marshall's gossip?' he prodded gently when she remained silent.

'I have eyes. I can see,' Dani murmured instead, afraid now to acknowledge the wild beat of her heart. 'And last night you were——'

'And last night I was escorting a future in-law of my family, nothing more,' Barrett finished the sentence for her, his gaze thoughtfully watching the betraying emotion on her face.

His thumbs were caressing the inside of her wrists, unsettling her already jumbled thoughts further. Dani's stomach was a mass of twisted, churning knots and there was a terrible urge to cry, because she couldn't understand what was happening to her.

'Now do you understand?' Barrett asked gently.

'No,' she answered weakly, closing her eyes briefly against the magnetic attraction. 'No, I don't understand anything.'

His smile was gentle, but it didn't relieve that peculiar ache in her chest. 'Sleep on it. I'll pick you up around eight in the morning.'

'Why?' numbed confusion in her face.

'Because I arranged to be free tomorrow and I want to spend the day with you.'

'But——'

'Eight o'clock,' he said firmly, releasing her wrists and touching a finger to her lips. Then he was walking away from her and seconds later Dani heard the door close.

Her arms wrapped themselves around her queasy stomach, a reaction she blamed on the news that Barrett wasn't serious about Nicole Carstairs. Although why that should be of such importance to her, Dani didn't know. She and Barrett were simply friends. That thought brought a sickening rush of pain.

A little voice inside her said, 'You aren't sick. You're in love.'

And Dani laughed aloud, a weak, tremulous laugh that soon caught in her throat. Love was a nebulous something that would come to her some time in the future. Not here! Not now! Not with Barrett King!

'Marshall. Why can't I be in love with Marshall?' she demanded, not realising she had spoken her thoughts.

But she wasn't. Tonight she had turned to Marshall for solace, to try to erase Barrett from her memory. Marshall's kisses had stimulated her, but it was Barret's brutal embrace that had wakened her desire against her will.

And Barrett? Did he simply feel responsible for her, as Marshall had said? Dani remembered again the control Barrett had exhibited during that embrace. Even her own father had asked him to see her so she wouldn't be alone. Yet it couldn't be strictly responsibility that made Barrett want to be with her, she argued. He had gone to great lengths to make her understand that Nicole meant nothing to him.

All those crazy, unanswered questions hammered to be heard until Dani's head pounded from trying to solve them. Then exhaustion swept over her again, this time draining her completely and mercifully, bringing an end to the questions she couldn't begin to answer.

With the morning sunlight they all came racing back. One moment her heart was leaping with the hope that Barrett might care and the next moment sinking to the deepest depths of despair against some imagined argument that he did not. By the time he arrived promptly at eight, Dani was as tense as a coiled spring, her brilliant gaze bouncing away from the levelness of his. In an effort to appear casual and uncaring, her mouth ran away with her tongue in a flurry of unnecessary comments while Barrett patiently sipped the coffee she had poured.

'Aren't you interested in where we're going today?' he asked, stopping her flow of trivia with a single question.

'Yes,' she swallowed, trying to glance his way casually and failing as her gaze slid rapidly back to her empty coffee cup.

'Good. I thought we'd take a drive through the country and I'll show you some of the attractions Kentucky has to offer besides Churchill Downs.'

'Would you like to leave now?' Dani asked nervously.

The slight reluctance in her voice earned her a quizzically amused look from Barrett. 'The sooner we leave, the more we'll be able to see.'

Her reply was a quickly worded agreement as she hurried to clear the coffee items from the table. Acid tears burned her eyes. Somehow she had hoped there would be some indication from Barrett of his feelings towards her after the way he had kissed her last night. Yet he was acting no differently from any of the other times he had taken her out. His friendly aloofness hurt.

The sheer futility of her love washed over her. Had it been so very long ago that she had asserted that they were no different? Now her clothes and appearance were impeccable. She had rubbed elbows with the élite of society and never in her life had she felt more certain that she wasn't good enough for a man such as Barrett King.

'Dani?' A hand touched her arm at the same moment that he spoke.

Her first instinct was to turn into his arms, accept the sweeping comfort of that broad chest. The impulse was so strong she had to jerk away from his touch to resist it, a creeping flush rising in her face when she looked at him. His eyes had narrowed and the line of his mouth had grown grim.

'You don't sound very excited about today.' There was an edge to his voice that cut Dani with its razor sharpness. Her throat refused to let any words pass through it. 'Is it because of last night?'

Her shoulders lifted in a defensive shrug. 'What are you talking about?'

She felt rather than saw the exasperated sigh from Barrett. 'Regardless of the impression I may have given you last night, I am not inviting you out with me today with a half-formed notion of seducing you. If I'd wanted to do that, I would have last night.' The shimmering green gaze was boring into the back of her neck. 'So forget about it.'

'That's not easy to do,' Dani admitted, knowing she would never forget and dying a little that he should ask her to do so. 'I don't know if we can be friends any more, Barrett.'

'It's always difficult for a man and a woman to be friends,' he said cryptically. 'But all we have to worry about today is enjoying ourselves.'

'Yes. Yes, of course,' she nodded, forcing a determined smile on her mouth.

'That's my girl,' Barrett said lightly, flashing her a quick smile before he turned away. It was a bittersweet phrase that Dani desperately wished was true.

She could read between the lines. Although Barrett recognised that it was impossible for them to go back to the easy relationship they had enjoyed before, his request to forget his violent lovemaking was a subtle statement that he did not want to become involved with her seriously. If he cared for her at all, it was because he felt obligated, indirectly responsible for the promise extracted by her father.

Proudly raising her chin, Dani vowed silently that Barrett would never guess the change in her feelings towards him. So she gave herself up to his lighthearted teasing mood and allowed him to believe the events of last night had been forgotten. What did it matter if her senses were too vividly aware of him beside her? The copper sheen of his hair. The bright glitter of his green eyes. The musically husky pitch of his voice. The intoxicating blend of cologne with his maleness. And the tantalising nearness of him behind the wheel of the car.

His tour through the Kentucky countryside surrounding Louisville took them first to Bardstown. Dani was grateful for the many things to see because they were able to fleetingly sidetrack her attention from Barrett. Tree-lined residential streets were crowned with stately mansions, including the home that had prompted Stephen Foster to write 'My Old Kentucky Home' while visiting Bardstown so many years ago.

Dani discovered she was even capable of laughter when they toured the Museum of Whisky History and saw an original whisky bottle distilled by E. C. Booz in 1854, a brand name that had prompted the present slang term of 'booze' for liquor.

The time passed more swiftly than Dani dreamed it could. When Barrett suggested a particular restaurant in Lexington for their evening meal, she could hardly believe that much time had gone by since lunch. The service was fast and excellent, leaving little time for small talk as she concentrated on the meal. There had been very little idle conversation the entire day, she realised. Both of them had kept the discussion centred on the sights they were seeing. Hers had been deliberate and she wondered if his had been, too.

'We should be able to make it home before dark,' she said idly after Barrett had paid the bill and they were on the way to his car.

'We aren't going back yet,' he said smoothly.

The velvetness of the coming night seemed so intimate that Dani bolted from the thought. 'Where are we going?'

'To the auction, of course. You haven't been to it before, have you?' There was an enquiring tilt to his head as he opened the car door for her.

'Auction?' Her mouth worked nervously before she got the word out.

'Don't tell me you haven't heard of the yearling sale

at Keeneland race-track before?' he chided mockingly.

The July sale of year-old Thoroughbreds Dani knew was heralded as the biggest and the best in the world. Horse breeders paid entry fees to have their colts and fillies considered for sale, but out of the thousand or so entries, only those yearlings with the bluest blood and the most desirable conformation were accepted.

And the buyers were just as élite. Tickets for seats in the sales pavilion were given only to those who could prove they could afford the five and six-figure price tag that the best yearlings in the land would fetch.

A shiver of excitement raced through Dani as she contemplated actually attending the auction of these untried and unnamed Thoroughbreds that could all trace their ancestry back to a handful of horses of the seventeenth and eighteenth century.

'I know all about the sale,' she murmured, the excitement dying. 'But I can't go, Barrett. You know that.'

'Because of your promise to your father,' he stated rather than asked.

'Yes,' she whispered. There was a funny ache in her throat and she had to look away from his solemn face.

'I don't see what the problem is,' Barrett shrugged. 'You can't possibly be breaking your promise by looking at a horse, unless you intend to buy one.'

His mocking rejoinder didn't succeed in raising a smile to erase her expression of helpless dismay. 'Please, take me home.'

'Dani, what are you going to do? Lock yourself in a

room?' he asked in a gentle kind of exasperation. 'Horses are everywhere. You can't spend the rest of your life avoiding their existence, whether it's a stable nag or a blooded stallion.'

'I know that's true,' Dani admitted, staring at her tightly clenched hands. 'But—Keeneland,' she sighed helplessly.

'Answer me honestly,' instructed Barrett firmly. 'Do you want to go?'

'That's beside the point,' she sighed again.

'It is the point,' he corrected. 'If you want to go, I'll take you. If you don't want to go, I'll take you home.'

'It isn't fair,' Dani protested. 'I want to go, but I won't break my promise to Lew.'

'Then I'm taking you to the sale.' His mouth closed in a grim line, ending any further discussion on the subject as he started the car and reversed out of the lot.

Secretly Dani was glad the decision had been taken out of her hands. Attending the Keeneland sale was a dream come true. She soothed the pricks of her conscience with Barrett's argument that looking at horses wasn't breaking her promise.

There was no longer any artificial sparkle to her smile as she and Barrett were whisked through the crowds of tourists outside the sales pavilion and into the select semi-circle of money green seats. The noise, the scattered conversation on the merits of this yearling over another the rustling pages in the catalogue, the raised dais of the auctioneer, his spotters stationed strategically around the arena, the electric excitement that crackled through the air, all these things Dani took in instantly.

Minutes later the auction began as the first colt was led into the roped enclosure beneath the auctioneer's stand, identified only by the number on his sleek hip. For the first few horses, Dani listened attentively to the singsong chant exhorting the buyers to go higher with their bids, and strained her eyes to catch sight of the bidders as they made their almost imperceptible signs, a flick of a finger, a bob of the head, the movement of a programme.

Slowly her mind began to shut out the murmurs of the crowd, the chant of the auctioneer, and the cries of the spotters. Not even the pressure of Barrett's shoulder against hers was noticed as she hypnotically studied the yearlings being led in, sold, and led out.

It was impossible to remain immune to the almost perfection of these prize horses, bred strictly for speed and beauty, the long, gracefully curved necks that swung up and down in cadence with the stride, propelling the horse forward, and the long, slender legs to increase the stride were the basic characteristics of the breed. But her father had taught Dani to look for the straight walk, the wide throat, muscular shoulders and haunches, and flat knees. As the hammer fell with the sale of the last horse, she leaned against the green back cushion, watching the milling crowds of buyers slowly exiting the arena.

'Are you sorry you came?' Barrett spoke for the first time since they had entered the sales pavilion.

She swallowed the tight lump in her throat. 'Yes, I am.' Her cinnamon-coloured eyes were misted over when she turned her gaze to him. The expression on his strong features showed no surprise at her answer.

'Why?' he asked, showing no inclination to move from his seat as his bland gaze swept over the taut lines of her face.

But Dani refused to answer, hunching instead a little deeper in her seat, cold arms of misery closing around her. Visions of those magnificent specimens of young Thoroughbreds danced in her head, bringing back haunting memories when racehorses had been such a vital part of her life.

'Have you finally realised that you have to live your own life?' he demanded. 'Not the one your father wants you to live? Or Marshall?'

'There's nothing wrong with being a model,' she dodged.

'Absolutely not, as long as that's what you want to be.'

'Why wouldn't I want to be a model?' she demanded with a defiant ring.

'That's something you'll have to decide for yourself,' Barrett replied calmly, rising to his feet and drawing her with him. 'Meanwhile I'll take you home.'

But Dani wasn't ready to let the subject be dropped. 'I suppose you still think I looked better when I ran around dressed like a boy with my hair cropped short and couldn't discuss anything except horses!'

His fingers bit into her upper arm as he spun her

around to face him. 'When will you stop degrading the girl that you used to be? There was nothing wrong with you. You were simply slower to mature owing to your background. In time, you would have awakened on your own to the feminine side of your nature.'

'So what are you saying?' Pain bit into her words as Dani remembered that slowly growing awareness she had felt about the way she dressed long before her father had ever pushed her out to become a woman. She could even admit that the antagonism Barrett had aroused in the past had been a defence mechanism to keep from falling under his spell. 'Are you saying I should go back to the track? Back to being a groom and an exercise boy?'

'I want you to do what you want to do, not what someone else tells you that you should do.' He released her arm and turned away.

'Why?' Dani asked in a beseeching kind of a whisper.

'Why what?' A brow lifted in enquiry.

'Why do you care?'

'Because I don't want to see you make a mistake and end up being unhappy,' Barrett said quietly.

'Is that why you've been seeing me? All those times,' she murmured, 'you were trying to protect me – like a big brother.'

There was an almost imperceptible movement of his head back and a cool aloofness stole into his eyes. 'Yes, that's basically right. You needed an anchor, some link with your past. I imagine I provided that for you.'

'I think your little sister has grown up now,' Dani said numbly, knowing he couldn't have made it plainer the way he regarded her.

'Have you?' returned Barrett, studying her thoroughly.

'At least I see things more clearly,' she stated, turning away so he couldn't see the bitter lines around her mouth.

The long drive back to Louisville was accomplished in silence. Dani didn't give Barrett a chance to accompany her to her apartment door as she burst quickly out of the car, thanked him for the day and told him quite firmly not to bother to come in. At the building entrance she didn't even turn around to wave.

The shrill ring of the telephone greeted her as she entered her apartment. Wearily, rubbing her aching head, she slumped on the couch beside the telephone and answered it.

'Danielle! My God! Where have you been?' Marshall's angry voice sounded in the receiver.

Not until that moment did Dani remember that Marshall had planned to come over this afternoon. 'I'm sorry, Marshall,' she answered insincerely. 'I should have let you know I would be gone.'

'I've been phoning all over town trying to find out where you were. Where were you?' he demanded.

She ignored the outraged tone of his voice and the question. 'Are you busy right now?' she asked instead. 'I'd like to come over.'

'Now?' Her request had plainly caught him by surprise. 'Is something wrong?'

'I'm not ill or hurt, if that's what you are thinking,' Dani laughed bitterly. 'I want to talk to you, and I'd prefer to do it tonight.' By morning her resolve might weaken.

'I'll be there in five minutes.'

CHAPTER TEN

'You've got to be crazy!' Marshall exclaimed when Dani broke the news to him. 'You're just beginning to achieve some success. You can't mean to quit now!'

'I can and I am,' she said emphatically.

'But why, for heaven's sake?'

'That doesn't concern you.' She sat down at the table and opened her chequebook, glad she had saved the money she had earned. Combined with the nest egg her father had given her, she had more than enough to pay back the money Marshall had expended. 'How much do I owe you?'

'You owe me a damned sight more than money!' His face darkened in anger.

'No, I don't. The only strings attached to you and me are monetary—a point you made yourself,' Dani reminded him firmly.

'At least you can tell me why you've suddenly decided that you're going to throw away everything I've given you!'

'It hasn't been sudden, Marshall, although it must seem that way.' A heavy sigh punctuated her statement. 'It's been building up subconsciously for quite a while. And today I realised this wasn't the way I wanted to live for the rest of my life. Oh, I admit that at first I found the newness of being a model and going to fancy parties exciting, rather like playing "dress-up". Lately I haven't enjoyed a minute of it.'

It was half-truths, all of it. But Dani was honest enough with herself to realise that it was Barrett King who had given her the majority of impetus to her decision. As long as she remained a model and a companion of Marshall's, Barrett would continue to see her, carrying on the big brother act that tore at the heart that loved him.

'I'm grateful for the help and support you gave me, Marshall,' she went on quietly.

'Oh, Danielle,' he moaned, his anger evaporating as he stared intently into her eyes, 'I can't let you go that simply. I want to marry you. You and I make a perfect team. We're perfect partners for one another.'

'You make it sound like a business merger.' A sad smile curved her mouth.

'I love you,' he hurried to assure her of that. 'We can take this town, this country by storm. Everyone will look at us and say "what a perfect couple".'

She could tell he meant every word that he said and she found that she felt a little bit sorry for him. 'What you don't understand, Marshall, is that I don't want that kind of a marriage. I don't want it to be a public thing, but a very private one with a home and babies.' A discovery she had realised only that moment, dark auburn-haired babies with green eyes. 'Would you want children?'

There was a puckering frown of hesitation between the dark brows before Marshall answered. 'If that was what you wanted,' he nodded.

'You always make the right answers,' she sighed, 'but it wouldn't work. I'm still a country girl, in spite of all the clothes and jewellery and make-up.'

Instinctively Dani knew that Marshall's feelings for her were only superficial. He was too interested in himself and his career to ever really fall in love. But he continued to argue the point, only accepting the cheque from Dani when she remained adamant in her stand.

When she finally persuaded him to leave, his last words to her were, 'I'm still going to get you to change your mind. John has a contract coming up for a fashion layout in a large magazine. You'll be in it.'

Dani smiled, 'Goodbye, Marshall.' And she closed the door.

What he didn't know, and she purposely hadn't told him, was that she wouldn't be here tomorrow to listen to his attempts, or any other day. First she was going to fly to New York where her father was. If he still didn't want her with him, then she would find somewhere else to go and something else to do. But she owed it to Lew to let him know that she didn't intend to keep the promise any more. Horses were in her blood just as they were in his, and becoming a social butterfly hadn't changed it.

While Barrett was letting her know that his feelings towards her were of a strictly brotherly kind, he had managed to make her understand that she couldn't keep that promise. With one hand he had taken away the hopes of realising one love and handed back her love of horses with the other.

The next morning, Dani bought suitcases and an airline ticket, closed her account at the bank and packed. It didn't matter that she might never have an opportunity to wear such beautiful clothes again. Never once did she allow herself to shed the tears that burned in her eyes. Her movements were silent and without haste as she ignored the ringing of the telephone and the doorbell. Not that there was any chance that Marshall could change her mind. She simply couldn't see any point in continuing the argument.

Hours later she stepped from the taxi cab that had taken her from the airport in New York to the Belmont race-track. Smoothing the wrinkles from the skirt of her yellow gold dress, Dani instructed the driver to help her place her baggage in one of the public lockers, paid him his fare and went in search of her father. She had taken particular care in her dress, wanting Lew to know that she had made the transformation from a tomboy into a young woman.

Her gaze eagerly searched the rows of stalls, the

sounds and scents welcoming her back. She saw several familiar faces, people she had met at other race-tracks. When she waved to them, they all waved back, but she could tell they didn't recognise her, a discovery that brought a wry smile to her face.

At the far end of a row of stalls, a sleek, mouse-grey horse stretched its neck towards her and whickered softly. Dani quickened her steps, her smile now one of pure gladness.

'Nappy!' she crooned softly as the stable pony affectionately butted his head against her shoulder. 'You didn't forget me, did you, old boy?' Her arms wrapped themselves around the grulla's neck, hugging him quickly before she remembered that she didn't want to soil the dress. She stepped back to fondle the horse's head.

'Is there something I can help you with, miss?' a voice asked behind her.

She turned slowly, her misty gaze tenderly wandering over the stocky man who had addressed her. 'Hello, Lew,' she said softly. At his vaguely bewildered expression clouded by recognition and uncertainty, she teased in a voice choked with emotion, 'Don't you recognise me?'

'Dani?' he questioned, his confused look giving way to glad amazement. 'Is it really you?'

'Yes,' she nodded eagerly.

'What are you doing here in New York?' Her father took one step forward, his arms reaching out to embrace her. Then he stopped, brushing a hand in front of his eyes as if he just remembered something. The happiness, the elation was gone from his voice when next he spoke, replaced by a controlled interest. 'You look wonderful! Every bit as lovely as I knew you would.'

Dani knew what was wrong. The promise. For a moment her head tilted down, her eyes studying the ground near her father's feet. Then proudly she met his gaze.

'I did what you wanted me to do, Lew,' she said with quiet determination in her voice. 'I've worn the latest fashions. I've attended the fanciest parties. I've eaten in the best restaurants. I've grown up, I'm a woman now.' She paused, unable to explain that falling in love with Barrett and suffering the pain of unrequited love had contributed more to her maturity than all of the other things. 'I've come back. I can't keep that promise, Lew. Horses and racing are in my blood just as they are in yours. And if you don't want me to be with you, then I'll find some other trainer to hire me.'

He blinked once, then twice, a tight smile curving his mouth. 'Welcome home, Dani,' he said gruffly, and held out his arms to her. Some minutes later he spoke again, still holding her tightly. 'I missed you so much, girl.'

Self-consciously Dani wiped the damp tears from her face. 'I missed you, too,' she sighed. 'And you never were a failure at anything.'

'How did you know where I was?' His hand affectionately ruffled her hair before he reluctantly held her away from him.

Her gaze fell beneath the warmth of his. 'Barrett King mentioned that he'd seen you here a couple of weeks ago,' she replied, wondering if the quiver in her voice when she spoke his name had betrayed her.

'He kept in touch with me,' Lew explained. 'Sent me clippings from the paper about you being at this party or that concert. I kept telling myself you were happy and I'd done the right thing, but it bothered me you being out there alone. I was feeling pretty sorry for myself when I sent you away. It took me a while to realise I had either to give up and die or fight back. The first didn't appeal to me, so I fought back. If Barrett hadn't been keeping an eye on you, I think I would have come and got you.'

'He . . . He was very kind.' Dani swallowed back the bitterness. It wasn't Barrett's fault that she had fallen in love with him. He certainly had never given her any encouragement. 'I wish you'd come for me, Lew.' Before I fell in love with Barrett, she added to herself, all the while knowing that it was probably inevitable anyway.

'Are you sure you want to come back with me?' he asked hesitantly, lifting her chin to gaze anxiously into her face. 'I've been doing better, but I'm still one step away from the poor-house. I mean, you're used to better things and a better way of life now.'

'But I wasn't happy,' she smiled lightly.

He stared at her for a long moment. 'Well then,' he

breathed deeply, a twinkle forming in his brown eyes, 'if you intend to feed those nags tonight, I think you ought to change into something more suitable.'

'Yes, sir,' she agreed gaily, snapping him a mock salute. 'I left my luggage at the public lockers. I'll go change right now!'

Returning to the routine of the racing stables was like putting on an old coat and finding it was still warm and comfortable. There were moments when Dani could almost believe that nothing had changed. Nothing around her had changed, but she had. True, she had gone back to wearing denim jeans and knit tops, but the schooling she had received from Giorgio and Marshall had taught her to choose colours and styles that would complement her face and figure. So now her curves were more attractively displayed and there was always a light application of make-up on her face.

She was quieter, not nearly as outspoken as she once had been—partly because of her own private heartache over Barrett, something she still wasn't able to confide to her father. Yet being back with horses, exposed to the excitement of race-days, lavishing care and attention on these blooded animals, Dani was almost able to convince herself that some day she would forget Barrett. Not soon, but in time.

Yet she dreaded the day when she would meet him again. And it was inevitable that she would, since his life was linked with horses and the track. Her only hope was that she would see him first and give herself time to prepare a suitably friendly but aloof attitude. She didn't try to convince herself that it would be easy. Even the casual mention of his name by her father sent her heart skipping beats and her mind conjuring up visions of his tanned face and the thick hair that captured the fire of the sun. Mostly it was his level green gaze, looking at her in that personal, thorough way that she found the hardest to forget and the impish twinkle that could coax a smile.

With a dispirited sigh, Dani leaned the pitchfork against the stall door, picked up the wheelbarrow partially filled with used straw and wheeled it down to the next stall. It was a hot muggy morning with little breeze stirring. The humidity had sapped her energy, but then, she shrugged as she unlatched the door and walked into the empty stall, cleaning stables had always been one of her least liked chores.

'You'll need the pitchfork,' a voice said from the open door.

Dani could neither move nor turn around. A hundred times she had heard that voice in her sleep. Like a tuning fork it seemed to vibrate through every nerve end. There was no opportunity to conceal the pain in her eyes as she slowly turned towards Barrett. Fortunately the dimness of the stall hid her tortured look. The sunlight streamed around him, accenting the height and breadth of of his silhouette.

'I should have guessed I would find you here,'

Barrett said grimly. 'There wasn't really anywhere else you could run to.'

'I didn't run,' Dani answered in a tautly defensive voice. 'I flew . . . in a plane.'

'Without telling a soul or leaving any kind of a message,' he snapped. 'Simply disappearing into the night. Didn't it occur to you that someone might be concerned?'

'The only one with any right to worry is Lew.' She had to hide behind her sarcasm. It was the only defence she had. 'I don't know what you're so upset about. I took your advice.'

'I didn't tell you to return to your father.' The severely controlled tone of his voice told her she was provoking his anger. 'And certainly not without telling someone.'

'Marshall knew,' she taunted him.

'He only knew that you were quitting. He had no idea of your destination,' Barrett said grimly.

'It wasn't his business, nor yours.' Dani deliberately made her voice cold and uncaring, a miracle considering the flooding heat that weakened her knees. 'I'm back with my father now, so you can drop the brotherly routine. Lew is all the family I want. I have no further need of your services.'

The knot in her chest was getting tighter and tighter. Each beat of her heart increased the pain until she wanted to die rather than face the rest of her life without Barrett.

'And I'm supposed to accept that?' he challenged.

'I don't care what you accept,' she cried, giving into the quick rush of pain. She breathed in deeply to regain control. 'Would you please give me the pitchfork and get out of here?' Her voice cracked. 'I have work to do.'

She could see the hesitation in his expression. She held her breath in fear that he would continue the conversation and she knew how brittle the thread was that held back her love. Then with a savage movement, Barrett tossed the pitchfork to her. She caught it in mid-air, thankful he hadn't made her walk across the stall to get it because she was certain her legs wouldn't have supported her.

Her eyes were already blurring with tears as she watched the impatient, angry strides that carried him out of the stall door. She leaned weakly against the pitchfork, silent racking sobs tearing at her body while the unbroken sunlight lay in a large rectangular square of gold at her feet.

This wasn't the time to give way totally to her heartbreak. Not here in the stables where anyone could walk by and question the reason for her tears. Resolutely Dani wiped them away, telling herself the worst was over. She had confronted him and hadn't lost control. One battle had been won, but the first victory was always the hardest.

Work was the answer. She must totally immerse herself in whatever she was doing, block out all but her subconscious thoughts of Barrett. Those she had no control over. With a vengeance she attacked the straw covering the stable floor, stabbing it with the pitchfork as if hoping to kill her love—a vain hope, but it served to release the frustration and anguish that twisted her insides.

With a pitchfork full of used straw and manure, Dani walked to the stall door to toss it into the wheelbarrow. There, leaning against the post supporting the wide overhang, stood Barrett, grim determination in his expression as his gaze flicked to her.

'What are you doing here?' Dani swallowed, searching for the sarcasm that had been her salvation before. 'I thought I told you to leave.'

In the clearness of the sunlight with none of the shadows from the darkened stall, the power of his attraction struck her like a physical blow. The carved teak brown of his powerful features, the dangerous glint in his eyes, that aura of sureness that he always got what he wanted.

'We still have more to discuss, Dani,' he stated. 'I was waiting until you'd finished your work.'

She averted her head from his compelling gaze. 'When I'm finished with this, I have plenty more to do.'

Her hands and arms were trembling now like her legs, making her attempt to shake the straw from the pitchfork awkward and unsuccessful. She wanted to scream from sheer frustration.

'Then I'll wait.'

'We haven't anything more to discuss.' Her voice

was very low, forced through the contracted muscles in her throat.

'Yes, we do,' Barret answered, unruffled by her effort to be rid of him. 'I want to take you to dinner tonight.'

'I thought I'd made it clear that it isn't necessary for you to see me any more,' Dani muttered. Her eyes were stinging again with acid tears that she refused to allow to surface as she concentrated her attention on the pitchfork. 'I'm back with Lew and your responsibility for me is over.'

'What time do you want me to pick you up?'

'Look here——' she began, turning her determined stance towards him and immediately regretting it as she came under the scrutiny of his disturbing and penetrating gaze. She had to pause to regain control. 'I'm ... I'm just a stable girl now. Surely you can find someone more worthy of the attention of the great Mr Barrett King.'

'That kind of sarcastic humility isn't going to change my mind,' he said calmly.

'Something had better change it,' Dani answered desperately, 'because I'm not going anywhere with you.'

A frown of determination creased his forehead. 'Simply because you're back with your father it doesn't suddenly end our friendship.'

'We aren't friends!' she retorted.

His brow lifted with mocking gentleness, a gesture meant to provoke a smile as he tilted his head enquiringly to one side. 'Not even bitter friends?'

The tender gesture evoked happy memories of more carefree times before she had fallen in love with him. They stabbed at her heart and forced her to turn away from the potent magnetism.

'Not even bitter friends,' Dani answered in a voice raw with pain.

Barrett sighed heavily and pushed himself away from the post he had been leaning against. 'Then come to dinner with me as my enemy.'

'No!' She spun around, dropping the pitchfork in the wheelbarrow and raising her hands in a beseeching plea. 'I want you to go away and leave me alone!'

'I can't do that. And I won't do that.' Barrett shook his head. 'If we have to go back to square one and start all over again, then that's what we will do.'

'Why?' Dani sighed despairingly. 'What good would it do?'

'Maybe I'll be able to make you trust me again.' The flash of anger in his eyes was turned inward on himself.

'Please. Please.' She was begging now and she didn't care at all about the loss of pride. 'Won't you leave things as they are—and leave me alone?'

'I could tell the next morning that I'd frightened you the night I burst into your apartment after seeing you with Marshall,' Barrett continued, taking a step closer to her as if he wanted to will her to understand. 'The only excuse I have is that I lost my temper. You were so naïvely certain that no man could force himself on you that I had to show you it was possible for your own good. I never meant to handle you so roughly.'

Dani gasped, swallowing back the bubble of hysterical laughter. It was so ironic that Barrett should be apologising for his actions that night. That night when she had discovered she loved him as only an adult woman can love a man.

'I don't blame you for hating me after the callous way I treated you,' he went on, stopping inches in front of her, 'but I swear I'll never give you cause to be frightened of me again.'

His broad chest was even with her head. His strong arms were at his side. Dani held herself rigid, fighting the temptation to seek the comfort of his embrace, the heart-stopping sensation of his body against hers. Clenching her hands into tight fists, she closed her eyes against his provocative nearness.

'Go away,' she pleaded, feeling the tears squeeze through her lashes. 'I don't want to see you any more.'

'I'm only asking for a chance,' Barrett persisted.

His hands closed lightly over her shoulders, the gentle touch snapping the thin thread that had held her motionless. A convulsive sob rose in her throat and this time Dani wasn't able to hold it back.

'No!' Her protest was feeble as her fists came up to hammer at his chest. The memory of that other time when she had tried to batter down the steel wall was completely forgotten. This time she only wanted to hit out at the man she loved so helplessly. The incessant pressure of his hands on her shoulders drew her against his chest, a movement designed to comfort the stream of tears flowing from her eyes.

Dani was torn by the desire to remain in the warmth of his arms and to break free. While her head refused to relax against the comforting solidity of his chest, her arms slid around his waist to cling to him tightly. The tortuous delight of his embrace shattered her restraint and her head bobbed in defeat.

'Please leave me alone, Barrett,' she moaned softly, her voice muffled by his shirt. 'Haven't you done enough already? Haven't I gone through enough agony without putting me through more? I couldn't help falling in love with you. I'll get over it in time, but only if you stay——'

Strong fingers were lifting her chin. She had a fleeting glimpse of his mouth descending before its mobile touch consumed her lips, wholly possessing and hungrily eager. With all her carefully constructed barriers gone, Dani responded. Her mind was reeling under the sensual shock waves of his kiss and she welcomed the crush of his arms, compelling her to yield to the hard contours of his body. Then came a darting moment of lucidity when she realised what she was doing and she tore herself free of his embrace.

Her eyes were wide and pleading as she gazed into his face, begging him not to shame her further by acknowledging the power she had placed in his hands. Her concern was so centred on that, Dani missed the exultant glitter in his eyes and the wondrous smile that raised the corners of his mouth.

'Go away, please,' she whispered fervidly, feeling like a wounded animal wanting to see some dark hole to hide in and lick her wounds.

'No,' Barrett answered softly, his gaze sweeping possessively over her as he reached out once more to grasp her unresisting shoulders. Dani had not the strength to struggle. 'I'm not going anywhere until you say that again.'

'Say what?' she breathed desperately, searching her mind for the words he wanted to hear that would set her free.

'Unless my mind is playing tricks on me, you just told me you loved me, didn't you?' His fingers unconsciously tightened as though to force her to admit it.'

'Oh, Barrett, I didn't mean to,' she moaned, casting her chin down to hide the anguish the admission caused. 'I know you never encouraged me. It isn't your fault that I made such a fool of myself.'

'You are a little fool!' he laughed. His hands slipped down to her waist and he raised her in the air lightly and easily. 'Don't you understand?' he smiled when he had once more set her on the ground and was gazing into her amazed face.

Dani felt she should hold her breath. It was too impossible to be true that Barrett actually meant what he was implying. 'No!' terrified of his answer.

His auburn head moved once again towards hers while he let his mouth roam over her face, exploring her eyes and cheeks. 'I love you, Dani,' he murmured against her skin.

The throbbing ache in his voice sent her pulse racing and her hands now lightly resting against his chest could feel the rapid hammer beat of his heart.

'Please, don't tease me, Barrett,' Dani murmured, her own lips beginning an intimate search of his face while her fingers curled into the thickness of the hair at the back of his neck.

'The way I feel for you is nothing to joke about,' he growled in mock anger, but she wasn't intimidated at all.

She nibbled gently at his mouth. 'I thought you only felt responsible for me—like a brother.'

'Those were Marshall's words, not mine. At first that was probably true,' he admitted, 'although I sometimes wonder if it ever was. That night when I carried you into bed and I kissed you, I knew I was kissing a woman and not an innocent young girl. The only problem was you hadn't realised that. I was afraid that if I showed you how much I cared I would frighten you. God,' he moaned, burying his head in the curve of her neck, 'that's what I thought I'd done.'

'You didn't,' Dani hurried to assure him, cradling his face in her hands. 'That night you discovered me with Marshall was the very night I realised I loved you. I probably had a long time before that—I always thought you were a handsome man. I never knew exactly why I didn't trust you, maybe it was because I knew you could steal my heart.'

'I guess turnabout is fair play, because you've stolen mine.' Barrett looked down at her and sighed, a happy sigh, one that her own heart echoed. 'I've wanted so long for you to meet my parents. I wanted to take you that weekend of their anniversary party, but I knew they would guess why I'd brought you. My father never could keep a secret, so I couldn't chance him letting something slip. I'll take you to the farm this weekend after we've had some time alone.'

'Barrett?' Her gaze was hesitant, an old fear rushing back to haunt her. 'About Melissa? You don't really think I'm like her, do you?'

'No.' His head moved to the side in a reassuring, negative movement. 'I did wonder if you would become blinded by the glamour Marshall had heaped on you. I wanted to tear you away from it, but I knew you had to have your chance. Lew was right about that.'

'What do you suppose Lew will say?' Dani asked, her eyes sparkling brightly as she gazed into Barrett's face, no more uncertainty in her mind that all of this was a dream.

'I don't think he'll be a bit surprised,' Barrett smiled widely, locking his arms about her waist. 'I had a little talk with him before I found you here at the stables. I'm positive he guessed that my interest was far from brotherly. My only hope is that he won't object to losing his only daughter when she'd only just returned to him.'

'Lew wants me to be happy,' she said, nestling

against his chest. 'I don't know which of us will be prouder, Lew to have you for a son-in-law or me to be your wife.'

'Are you asking me to marry you?' Barrett teased.

'You always said I was a cheeky brat,' she smiled demurely.

'Mmm,' he said, teasing her lips with his mouth. 'Well, the answer is yes. I will marry you, and the sooner the better.'

His arms tightened around her and Dani understood. The ache in her own body couldn't long be ignored either.

'I love you so much,' she declared in a whispering vow, and brought her lips to his to seal their pledge.

CLAIM THE Crown

Carla Neggers

The complications only begin when they mysteriously inherit a family fortune.

Ashley and David. The sister and brother are satisfied that their anonymous gift is legitimate until someone else becomes interested in it, and they soon discover a past they didn't know existed.

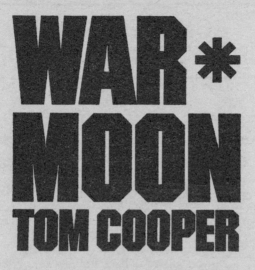

Harlequin Historical Romance

COME AND MEET
OUR HISTORICAL HEROES!

Whether it be

- a fabulously wealthy captain in Regency England
- a dark prince of the Welsh in the Middle Ages
- a notorious and ruthless pirate roaming the British high seas
- or many other wonderful men awaiting you each month in Harlequin Historical Romance

With them you will travel back in time...experience different life-styles, high adventures, exciting challenges—with love always the most glorious of them all.

Every month, ask for the two Harlequin Historical Romance titles at your favorite bookstore.

Don't miss any of them!

ATTRACTIVE, SPACE SAVING BOOK RACK

Display your most prized novels on this handsome and sturdy book rack. The hand-rubbed walnut finish will blend into your library decor with quiet elegance, providing a practical organizer for your favorite hard-or soft-covered books.

Only $9.95

**Approximately
16" x 8"
when assembled**

Assembles in seconds!

To order, rush your name, address and zip code, along with a check or money order for $10.70* ($9.95 plus 75¢ postage and handling) payable to *Harlequin Reader Service*:

> Harlequin Reader Service
> Book Rack Offer
> 901 Fuhrmann Blvd.
> P.O. Box 1325
> Buffalo, NY 14269-1325

> *Offer not available in Canada.*

*New York residents add appropriate sales tax.

BKR-1R